Praise for *The Rose Ci*

"David Ebershoff... author of a .... novel last year, *The Danish Girl*, returns with an excellent collection of seven stories. 'Regime' is one of the best, rawest gay stories I have ever read. Let's hope the Modern Library can spare [Ebershoff] for the occasional sabbatical. His ... is beginning to be an important body of work about American life on the sexual margins, a talented and welcome addition to the gay literature canon." —*Chicago Tribune*

"What is striking soon into *The Rose City* is David Ebershoff's exceptional talent as a stylist. The prose in every one of the seven short stories in the collection is refined without being precious, intricate though never overwrought, elegant and yet capable of being taut when necessary. Ebershoff loves words like poets do, and he makes good use of them. There is a rhythm to his sentences that is also akin to poetry. In a way the perfect review from this book would simply quote passages from it, the vivid descriptions of landscape, the insightful depiction of characters, the impressive evocation of moods and atmospheres. No doubt this is as strong a collection as you will read all year." —*The Denver Post*

"Emotional fiction can certainly hit home sometimes. This is one of those books whose situations float around in your personal space long after you read them. In *The Rose City*, David Ebershoff's fictions map the angst-ridden dreams of his characters with an experienced, compassionate eye, and the result becomes as tragic, beautiful, and rose-red as life itself." —*Bay Area Reporter*

"*The Rose City* will not disappoint Ebershoff's admirers. These stories are marked by the same stylistic elegance, gentle humor and adept storytelling that distinguished the writer's first novel. Despite their similarities in theme and setting, the stories in *The Rose City* offer an array of distinct, well-developed characters. The intriguing situations and characters in *The Rose City* are matched by Ebershoff's finely crafted prose. He has a precise, often humorous eye for detail, capturing some aspect of character or place with a single phrase. This collec-

tion demonstrates the same assurance in the short story that Ebershoff manifested so abundantly in his first novel."
—*The Atlanta Journal-Constitution*

"Intimate, imaginative . . . Ebershoff creates painful, private worlds alive with yearning. And what these characters yearn for is just as vivid . . . Ebershoff's stories are at once precise and expansive. Ebershoff has been heaped with all manner of high praise in the past few years, and *The Rose City* confirms his status as one of the best short story writers in America in whose work little moments of epiphany come fast and furious."
—*Philadelphia Weekly*

"Anyone who read David Ebershoff's spellbinding 1999 novel *The Danish Girl* knows of this writer's dark, intense prose style and themes of complex sexuality. . . . *The Rose City* . . . has the same unsettling power as his novel."
—*The Baltimore Sun*

"True to the form he established in his first novel *The Danish Girl* . . . Ebershoff is on a roll and is gathering a following of fans who gravitate to his quirky characters . . . the author's talent is obvious."
—*Pasadena Star-News*

"Twitchy with life . . . crystalline, beautifully drawn narratives . . . [Ebershoff is] a lyrical and artful writer."
—*San Francisco Bay Guardian*

"[A] winning collection of stories. . . . The acclaimed author of *The Danish Girl* is especially adept at exploring lives on the sexual precipice."
—*The Advocate*

"Most of the stories have a tragic edge, their protagonists mired in frustrations and obsessions, but Ebershoff capably draws readers into their lives. . . . Ebershoff delivers a bouquet of vivid, hard-edged characters plagued by all-too-human frailties."
—*Publishers Weekly*

"Ebershoff employs sensitivity and compassion in these intriguing and emotionally charged short stories."
—*Library Journal*

PENGUIN BOOKS

THE ROSE CITY

David Ebershoff is the publishing director of the Modern Library, a division of Random House, Inc. His first novel, *The Danish Girl*, was published to widespread acclaim around the world and won the Rosenthal Foundation Award from the American Academy of Arts and Letters and a Lambda Literary Award. He is a graduate of Brown University and the University of Chicago, and has taught fiction writing at New York University and has been a Lecturer in the Council of Humanities at Princeton. His most recent book is the novel *Pasadena*. Originally from California, he now lives in New York City and can be reached at www.ebershoff.com.

THE
ROSE
CITY

STORIES

David
Ebershoff

PENGUIN BOOKS

PENGUIN BOOKS
Published by the Penguin Group
Penguin Putnam Inc., 375 Hudson Street, New York, New York, 10014, U.S.A.
Penguin Books Ltd, 80 Strand, London WC2R 0RL, England
Penguin Books Australia Ltd, 250 Camberwell Road, Camberwell,
Victoria 3124, Australia
Penguin Books Canada Ltd, 10 Alcorn Avenue, Toronto,
Ontario, Canada M4V 3B2
Penguin Books India (P) Ltd, 11 Community Centre, Panchsheel Park,
New Delhi – 110 017, India
Penguin Books (N.Z.) Ltd, Cnr Rosedale and Airborne Roads,
Albany, Auckland, New Zealand
Penguin Books (South Africa) (Pty) Ltd, 24 Sturdee Avenue, Rosebank,
Johannesburg 2196, South Africa

Penguin Books Ltd, Registered Offices:
Harmondsworth, Middlesex, England

First published in 2001 by Viking Penguin,
a member of Penguin Putnam Inc. 2001
Published in Penguin Books 2002

10 9 8 7 6 5 4 3 2 1

The following stories were previously published in slightly different form:
"Chuck Paa" in *Genre* and *Best American Gay Fiction 2*, edited by Brian Bouldrey (Little, Brown); "The Dress" in *Puerto del Sol*; "The Charm Bracelet" in *Genre*; "Living Together" in *Christopher Street*; "The Rose City" in *Harrington Review*; and "Trespass" in *Alligator Juniper* and *Men on Men 6*, edited by David Bergman (Plume).

LIBRARY OF CONGRESS HAS CATALOGED THE HARDCOVER EDITION AS FOLLOWS:
Ebershoff, David.
    The Rose City and other stories/David Ebershoff.
       p. cm.
    Contents: Chuck Paa—The dress—Living together—The charm bracelet—Regime—The Rose City—Trespass.
    ISBN 0-670-89483-4 (hc.)
    ISBN 0 14 20.0081 7 (pbk.)
    I. Title.
PS3555.B4824 R67 2001
813'.54—dc21   00-052756

Printed in the United States of America
Set in Scala
Designed by Carla Bolte

For Jack Woody

Like all children, I led a double life.

—William Trevor

CONTENTS

THE ROSE CITY

CHUCK PAA

Chuck Paa, five and a half feet tall, his eyes gold and set deep beneath the brow, asked, "What do you need, Mr. Boyal? Chips? Cake mix? Corn oil? Where's your shopping list? Get out your list."

Mr. Boyal, glasses slipping down his nose, pointed to the breast pocket of Chuck's parka. Only a quarter of an hour before Chuck had picked up the list from the telephone table next to Mr. Boyal's front door, zipping it into the parka and patting the flap for good measure. Then Chuck had forgotten all about it. He must have been thinking of something else at the time: his paycheck arriving in tomorrow's mail; the red-and-black HELP WANTED sign in the window of the liquor store; the call he needed to place to Mr. Riley. Yes, something.

Now Mr. Boyal was leaning heavily on the shopping cart as he pushed it down the baked-goods aisle. It rolled slowly, its back wheels trembling, until Mr. Boyal seemed to lose track of what he was doing, steering the cart into a display pyramid of canned pickled beets. The pyramid collapsed on itself with an extended clatter, and Chuck Paa tried to look the other way.

But worse than the racket of the cans rolling down the aisle was the sight of Mr. Boyal himself. His knees were wobbling, his blue hand was grasping the cart's handle, and Mr. Boyal was on the verge of crumbling into a heap. Here we go again, thought Chuck, moving to catch Mr. Boyal. More than once Chuck had told him it was time to buy a walker, preferably the kind with the little white skis. But Mr. Boyal had—as Chuck expected—resisted. Yet when Chuck mentioned the walker to Mrs. Boyal, Mr. Boyal's sad-mouthed mother who lived far away in Pasadena, her tongue snapped across the phone line. "I couldn't agree more. I just didn't have the heart to bring it up myself." "Well, I have the heart," Chuck replied. And Mrs. Boyal, with her poof of silver-blond hair and pinched oily nose, said, "Oh, Chuck. Aren't you kind to us all."

"Here, Mr. Boyal," Chuck said at the bakery counter. "You like sugar cookies, don't you? They're on sale this week, only five cents each. Two bucks will get you enough for a week." Chuck placed the sack of clover-shaped cookies into the cart's baby seat. His hand, which was a small hand, even Chuck knew, scampered into the sack and pushed a cookie to his mouth. And then Chuck snapped his fingers, wet with saliva and decorated with green sprinkles, and he realized this: He had asked Mr. Boyal *where's the list?* to test his mind. Dementia was so common, after all.

But that wasn't the real reason, Chuck knew. No, the real reason was he'd simply forgotten what he'd done with it, thinking of something else.

"What's next?" Chuck glanced at the grocery list and directed Mr. Boyal to the seafood counter. Mr. Boyal liked to order his fish on his own, and so Chuck Paa leaned against the Mexicana rack that clutched bags of tortilla chips and jars of green-pepper salsa and pull-top tins of refried beans. Mr. Boyal's hair, yellow but somehow colorless, lay flatly on his skull. It hadn't been like that when Chuck began working for him. No, Mr. Boyal had once possessed a full set of hair, or almost. His face, too, had passed from man to cadaver before Chuck's eyes: cheeks as deep as saucers now, and this morning some sort of infection curdling white in his eyes; Chuck had had to take the damp corner of a tea towel to dab them clean.

Even so, Chuck had seen worse.

Mr. Boyal worked the numbered paper pennant out of the dispenser. His fingers, all bone, fluttered, tugging on the bit of blue paper. He held it up, showing Chuck that he was 43, four behind Mrs. 39 who now was ordering tuna steaks from the fish man, chattering about how the Star Market's fish prices were becoming *insupportable*. "Your prices are higher than they've ever been!"

That was it!

Chuck had forgotten what he'd done with the list because he'd been thinking of Ben. On his way to Mr. Boyal's this morning, he ran into Ben in front of the liquor store. Six months had passed since Chuck had seen him, a period of time that had quickly but thoroughly picked away at Ben's health: wrists thin and nearly strangled by the kudzu vines of his veins; skin scaly and a clammy gray; a colony of white nodules on his throat, like little toadstools. For the first time he had spent a night in the hospital, Ben reported breezily, as if it were a rite of passage, as if Chuck had known all along Ben had been ill.

"Did you have a nice room?"

"It was okay," said Ben. "Say, who are you working for these days?"

"Mr. Boyal."

"Jimmy Boyal? Right here on Columbus?"

"Mr. Boyal? You know Mr. Boyal?"

"Sure. He's an old friend."

"Mr. Boyal is an old friend of *yours*?" asked Chuck, who was heating up under his parka. "Maybe it's a different Mr. Boyal. My Mr. Boyal has blond hair and a tiny little chicken pox scar just here."

Chuck Paa touched his face.

"That's Jimmy." Ben giggled slightly, as if something were a secret. "But I haven't seen him in over—"

But Chuck stopped listening. He studied Ben from the corner of his eye. With his cold skin and his unsteady gait, Ben looked as though he might need a helper sometime soon. A pang entered Chuck's chest as he realized he couldn't offer his services to Ben as long as he worked for Mr. Boyal. And so

Chuck, who was about to be late, said, "Maybe you'll stop by and visit Mr. Boyal someday." He added, "We—he—would love a visitor." And then, this time with a wrinkle of pain in his voice, "You're managing on your own? You can still do everything on your own, can't you, Ben?"

As the fish man called number 43, Mr. Boyal cheerfully waved the tag of paper. Chuck smiled at his employer and then began to pick at the rim of his face. At twenty-three Chuck's pores had yet to abandon their adolescent flow of grease and grime. The quality of his skin remained immature and frustratingly clogged. Not that he thought of it that way: No, in fact he was more obsessed with his skin than that, finding its condition both better and worse than it actually was. And despite his best efforts—the bar of Lifebuoy soap, the washcloth worn bald, the straight-up rubbing alcohol—Chuck knew no one would ever examine his skin and comment on its healthy glow. On Tremont Street he felt as if the young men could see only the oily dents in his face, tar pits he called them, though if pressed Chuck would have to admit that was an exaggeration. *Boyz*, the young men called themselves, men with laundered dress shirts and tassel loafers, their faces perpetually lit from a step aerobics class and a steam at the Metropolitan Gym. Not that they were the only ones roaming the South End, though sometimes it felt that way. No, there were others, women and families and shopkeepers and meter maids, and the clutch of ghostly men who ventured out with trembling canes. Just like Mr. Boyal, who was still waiting, his neck dewy and draining of color, for the fish man to wrap up his perch. Or Ben, who had waved good-bye with an awkward plea in his cloudy eyes.

Seeing Mr. Boyal blanch even more, Chuck asked if he

wanted to sit, although Chuck couldn't think where Mr. Boyal might rest in a supermarket. On the little bench in front of the fish counter where the loaves of French bread were stacked like sandbags? In the shopping cart itself?

Chuck had never trained as a helper, nor as a boy had he imagined that this was how he'd pass his days. He had no particular inclination for this sort of profession—all this fussing over men who could no longer fuss over themselves. But work was work—his heart still quickened whenever he heard that inimitable *rip!* of a check being yanked from its book—and now he could no longer picture himself doing anything else. The pay was good, and in these bleak times of raging plague the jobs so bountiful that Chuck's biggest problem was deciding who to work for and how to regretfully say no; nothing balled him up more than having to turn down a chance to earn another dollar. When he was eighteen he abandoned his Finnish-blooded mother in her two-room apartment in Maine and moved to Boston. Out of the woods and into the big city: That was how he liked to think of it, even though he'd grown up on a rough street in Portland. Upon arrival, he walked from the bus station to the Charles River, then cut across into the South End: Columbus Avenue, St. Cloud's, the Purple Iris flower shop, a corner bookstore with a neon rainbow in the window. When Chuck saw a man talking to another with a goatee and a little white dog, Chuck knew to stop. This was the place. These were the men— or the *Boyz*—he was meant to live among. His next thought was of work—of survival, really—and he eyed the storefronts for HELP WANTED signs: a video rental, an ice-cream counter, a wine shop that also hawked baskets of tube cheese. Under closer inspection, the awning of the Purple Iris flower shop flapped in the breeze with a gash through its canvas, and the buckets in the refrigerated window sat half empty, and there was a sheet of paper taped to the door that said: GOING OUT OF BUSINESS! EVERY-THING FOR SALE. You see, Chuck had arrived in Boston during the recession a few years back, and not a single window displayed a HELP WANTED sign. Yet this moment of panic—*How will I feed myself? Where will I sleep?*—was not the first to clamp its clammy cuff around Chuck's wrist; no, Chuck had wondered before—and he somehow knew he would wonder again—from what dented pot would he scrape his next meal.

When he was thirteen, his mother, a shoplifter who had trouble holding a job, took a position as a summer maid at a house on a private island named Little Thule two hundred yards off the coast of Maine. After school let out in May, she and Chuck settled into a room with sloped walls above the house's stable. There were five girls in the family who summered on the island, and a boy a year older than Chuck named Bennett. After a few days, Bennett, eager to get away from his sisters, turned to Chuck for friendship, offering him his Red Sox cap when he saw Chuck squinting and his face burning in the clear blank summer light. From then on Bennett took Chuck clamming and fishing for scrod and out on his gray-planked dory, *Bennett Boy,* to pull up the island's lobster pots. Bennett, with his long brown feet and the downy tendril of hair on the nape of his neck, taught Chuck to clean a cod and to rinse the black waste from a mussel. Almost every day the boys would dirty themselves with lobster tomalley and the blood of alewife. Or they would rake the manure in the pony ring and then, together, ride the old horse, Danny

Boy, round and round. Or they would paint the peeling toolshed wearing nothing but gym shorts, their backs becoming speckled with the splatter of paint—to say nothing of the time Bennett silently painted bright white circles around Chuck's hardening nipples and then a thin upturned smile beneath his navel. Each evening Mrs. Wriston, Bennett's sun-damaged mother, would direct the boys with her talonish finger to the claw-footed tub in the service bathroom. "Soak for as long as it takes," she'd demand, latching the door behind her, leaving them to the moist-aired room with the pillowy towels. Chuck would eagerly yank himself out of his soiled clothes, except the Red Sox cap, and plop into the tub where he'd sit knee-to-knee with Bennett. It was what Chuck liked most, even more than the fishing or the horseback riding or painting the toolshed. The steamy water. The lavender-scented soap. The red sponge in the shape of a heart that Bennett used to scrub Chuck's back. "Boys are allowed to wash each other's backs," Bennett would say, his whispering voice growing deeper almost by the day, his fingertips carefully picking away at each whitehead of paint until Chuck was clean, his body pink, and his child's fist of a heart swollen. Every night they bathed together, their hands interlocked, their faces becoming as clean and shiny as plates, and Chuck found it remarkable that everyone—his small-faced mother, Mrs. Wriston with her dug-in eyes, but especially Bennett himself—thought it was the most natural thing in the world for each day to end like this. And so Chuck came to believe this was how things were meant to be: the direct summer sunlight, the cold green ocean, the friendship grounded equally in solidarity and intimacy. Chuck could look no further than the present, his memory forgetting where he'd come from, how he'd arrived here, and his imagination suddenly unable to envision, or plan for, his future, his own survival. But then one humid morning in August Mrs. Wriston witnessed Mrs. Paa, with desperation permanently etched across her forehead, snatch a dolphin-shaped brooch from her mother-of-pearl jewelry box. Within hours Chuck and his mother were ferried off the island while Bennett sat on the anchored bow of *Bennett Boy*, his feet dangling into the dimpled water, his valentine face following the heads of Chuck and Mrs. Paa thirty feet away as the outboard motorboat captained by Mrs. Wriston herself puttered toward the rocky, pocked shore. *You'll come back,* Bennett's face seemed to be saying. Pretending a lifting breeze had come along, Chuck knocked his Red Sox cap into the boat's wake—as if to say, *Yes, I'll come back. Never again with her, but I'll come back.*

Now Mr. Boyal was nudging Chuck and saying, "Daydreaming on the job? Chuck, are you there?" And then, "Just perch today." Mr. Boyal attempted a smile. "I don't think I need anything else."

"Check your list, Mr. Boyal." He handed him the piece of paper.

Mr. Boyal noted each item. "I still need a vegetable."

"Creamed spinach is on sale." Chuck held up the supermarket's circular. He paused. "I didn't know you're friends with Ben, Mr. Boyal."

"Ben?"

"Ben who lives on Dartmouth Street."

"Oh, Ben." His nose twitched. "I wouldn't say we're friends. Did you once work for him?"

"Not exactly," Chuck said, feeling the blood rise to his face.

Since January Chuck had worked for Mr. Boyal as a daily companion, helping him shop and cook and, when the weather was bright, taking him for a stroll through the Commons. Really, his tasks required very little skill; it was all that ordinary and mindless. Not that people didn't appreciate all that he did—that was how they put it. Not that people didn't commend him in low, whispery voices for *all that he did*. Mrs. Boyal, who smelled like honey and tied little flowered scarves around her throat, shook his hand the time she flew out from California to check up on Mr. Boyal. She always enclosed a note on an ecru card when she mailed his checks, one of which was due tomorrow. Such fuss people made over keeping track of a dying man's grocery list.

At the checkout counter, Mr. Boyal turned and said, "Why don't I make you lunch today?"

Chuck nodded. Mr. Boyal prepared lunch every day. It was an exercise, and Chuck liked almost anything Mr. Boyal made, except the spinach salad. He especially loved the pink cupcakes decorated with rainbow sprinkles.

For almost a year now, Jerry Riley, the brother of one of Chuck's previous clients, had been asking Chuck to work for him. He owned a liquor distributorship that specialized in imported beers. It was a business of relationships, he once told Chuck, and Mr. Riley saw him as the man who could get his beers into all the gay bars from Portland to New Haven. But why Chuck Paa? You seem like a loyal young man, Mr. Riley had said. You don't seem like the type who'd think about screwing me over. Mr. Riley also admitted he himself would never set foot in a gay bar, but that wasn't a reason to walk away from money on the counter. The first time he made the offer was nearly a year ago, at the wake of Harold Riley, who died in his sleep, boiled over with fever. "Do it for old Harry," Mr. Riley had said, filling his mouth with an aunt's deviled egg. Although flattered, Chuck declined; there were others on a list waiting for his services. Mr. Riley probably took a liking to Chuck because in his final months Harold's life insurance money had run dry, leaving him with little to pay Chuck, and yet Chuck had stayed on, each morning walking over to Harold's narrow apartment on West Newton Street, opening the front door with the worn brass key he protected on a string around his neck. He would feed Harold's two tabby cats and then wake Harold himself, shaking the knob of his shoulder until his papery eyelids began to flutter, which would tell Chuck that today was not the day—his responsibilities would continue. For nine weeks Chuck repeated this routine without pay, each morning rising earlier and earlier as Harold's body shut down more and more, so that Chuck started arriving at Mr. Riley's even before the tabby cats had risen themselves. For two months this had meant that Chuck could never buy the three coconut doughnuts he liked in the morning; it meant no groceries except cans of black beans and pickled beets, on sale because of a dent in the tin; it meant no replacement when his bottle of shampoo emptied; and after a month it meant no quarters for the hungry, humming machines at the Tidy-Tide laundromat. All this Chuck bore not out of kindness but out of *duty*, a sense of professionalism, an approach to survival deliberately in contrast to his mother's. When Chuck began working for someone, he always made a promise to himself that he'd never leave his client until his client left him. And so Chuck continued to work—his body thinning and dirtying at an exponential pace—until the morning he arrived at Harold's apartment only to find the two tabby cats nudging their orange, delicate bodies against the cold, dead wall of Harold's now peaceful chest.

Two weeks later Jerry Riley phoned to inform Chuck that Harold had left him a gold pocket watch, which Chuck quickly pawned. Jerry Riley had also said, "I mean it about the job. Stay in touch with me, Paa. I could be your ticket out."

Chuck asked Mr. Boyal what he would make for lunch today. "For some reason I'm extra-hungry," Chuck said as they walked from the supermarket to Mr. Boyal's parlor-level apartment in the South End.

"I'll broil the perch."

"How about frying it in the canola oil?"

"Maybe," Mr. Boyal said, already tiring from his sack of groceries. He set it on a cement stoop, and suddenly a fit of coughing hurled up from his lungs and bent him at his waist. A tick of worry bit into Chuck. How long would his assignment with Mr. Boyal last? Would they be together come summer?

"Give me a minute," Mr. Boyal said, sitting on the stoop. Chuck sat down, too, his hot wet hand with the wadded grocery list touching, lightly, Mr. Boyal's back.

The two men shut their eyes.

"Catch your breath yet, Mr. Boyal?" Chuck asked. "Ready to move on?" As he carried the groceries down the street of brownstones, Chuck was thinking about working for two people at once. Ben had said he didn't need any help. Maybe not now, but perhaps in a few months when Mr. Boyal. . . . Chuck calculated the business of it, the potential and the limits for profit. If only he could duplicate himself, make a team of Chuck Paas, and care for Mr. Boyal and Ben at once—then that would be worthwhile. He shifted the grocery bags in his fists as the sweat began to collect inside his parka. He watched Mr. Boyal's neck, just a twig really, move inside the yawning collar of his sweater. Chuck saw a DRIVERS NEEDED sign painted on the back of a delivery truck and told himself to remember the 1-800 number, though he knew he'd forget it in an hour. And then Chuck, whose skin was mushroom-white in the weak spring sun, silently watched the grocery list slip from beneath the shopping bag's plastic handle pressing into his palm, the list delicately floating away from a sticky starfish of a hand that seemed to belong to someone else, that seemed not to belong to Chuck Paa at all.

———

The next day Chuck took Mr. Boyal for a haircut. Waiting on a bench padded with magazines, Mr. Boyal said, "I have an appointment with a nutritionist tomorrow."

"Why?" Chuck was flipping through a men's fashion magazine, imagining the two-tiered haircuts first on himself and then on Mr. Boyal.

"I'm not sure I'm eating as well as I should."

"Who told you that?"

"Ben." Mr. Boyal was sitting erect with his back straight and his hands cupped over the handle of his cane, and Chuck could feel Mr. Boyal's eyes move curiously across him. Had Mr. Boyal and Ben spoken about Chuck last night? "Ben's had some success with macrobiotics."

"I see," said Chuck, wondering if Ben would share his

recipes and the name of a good health food store—for a lump had begun to rise in Chuck's throat when he thought that he might not have been feeding Mr. Boyal properly. Or was the lump from something else?

Just last week Chuck rode the T down to Braintree to see Mr. Riley in his office in a blue-roofed warehouse. Mr. Riley, who was hairier than Chuck Paa but not much taller, gave him a tour of the floor. While Mr. Riley explained his inventory management system, Chuck's eyes stopped on a truck driver with a spiky crew cut. The driver was wearing blue overalls and a sewn-on patch that said *Eugene*. As he loaded the shelves of a truck with cases of beer, his arms flexed with strings of muscle, causing a sway in Chuck's chest. Mr. Riley slapped Chuck's back and said that, were he to come on board, Eugene would deliver to any of the routes Chuck could develop. He knew he was gaping; he had to quickly bring a handkerchief to his chin to catch the lurching drop of drool that, as it turned out, wasn't actually there. "Anything wrong, Chuck?" said Mr. Riley. "You seem a little nervous about something." Even so, he still wanted Chuck as part of his operation. I've got a feeling about you, he told Chuck Paa.

"Thinking of anything different for the hair?" Chuck asked Mr. Boyal.

"No, I wasn't. Any suggestions?"

"Ever have a back rub?" a blind client had once asked Chuck Paa. His heart began to thump so rapidly with hope that he was certain the man could hear its patter from across the living room. Other than his sight, the man's health was holding up, and all Chuck was doing for him was driving him on errands once or twice a week. "Not since I was thirteen," Chuck replied, lying down, feeling the slab of his stomach seep into the cracks between the sofa cushions. "Your shirt off?" the man asked playfully, approaching the couch. But then Chuck, fearing the state of his skin, told the man to forget about the massage.

"They're calling you, Mr. Boyal," Chuck said.

"No, they're not. They just called a Mr. Doyle."

After the haircut Chuck walked Mr. Boyal back to his apartment. It was a warm, early spring afternoon, and sweat began to roll down their foreheads. Once inside, Mr. Boyal, his face ashen, set himself on the plaid sofa while Chuck went to the kitchen for some water. When he returned he found Mr. Boyal slumped on the couch like an overturned sack, a trail of foam spilling from his mouth. Uh-oh, Chuck thought, hoping Mr. Boyal hadn't gone off and died on him just then. Had he walked Mr. Boyal too hard? Would they blame him? He nervously placed his thumb to Mr. Boyal's pipe of a wrist, locating a pulse. Chuck fell to Mr. Boyal's side in relief. After catching his breath, Chuck turned to Mr. Boyal and slapped his icy face. He didn't come to. Chuck telephoned an ambulance and then Mr. Boyal's doctor at Mass General. Then Mrs. Boyal in Pasadena. Chuck Paa wasn't naturally levelheaded in a crisis, but Mr. Boyal had penned instructions of what precisely to do should he teeter over. And thank goodness! Chuck had demanded that everyone he worked for do the same, even those he only helped out for an afternoon: Should you pass out or die while under my watch, please write down exactly how you would like me to react. Chuck supplied the pen and the index cards.

Mr. Boyal spent two nights in the hospital. When he came

home, Mrs. Boyal, who had jetted in, announced in her girlish voice that the time had come to move Mr. Boyal back to Pasadena. Chuck hadn't planned on leaving Mr. Boyal for several months, and no one else had offered him a full-time position. Although Mrs. Boyal ceremoniously sent Chuck off with a three-week bonus and a white mum in a clay pot, it was the first time since he had arrived in Boston that he'd found himself out of work. He still had some onesy-twosy jobs—helping with a move, special errands, baby-sitting for an evening. Mr. Boyal said he would send out word among his friends that Chuck was available, but the trouble was (though Chuck Paa didn't say this) most of Mr. Boyal's friends were dead.

When it was time for good-byes, Chuck said, "Keep me posted." He meant both about Mr. Boyal's health and any job prospects.

"I will," said Mr. Boyal. After his stay in the hospital, where they cleaned a parasite out of his intestine, he looked fitter than Chuck had ever seen him, his eyes clear and alert and color returned to his cheek. Mr. Boyal reported on some sort of new combination therapy that was showing good early results; something to do with an inhibitor of some sort or another. He was carrying a blush of hope in his face, standing erect to see Chuck off, and who was Chuck Paa to tell Mr. Boyal that there was no hope at all? Chuck believed in a cure about as much as he believed the world would one day be his own.

"When I find something," Chuck asked, as he always did at the end of an assignment, "can I use you as a reference?"

"If I'm still around." A smile broke open his face. Was that a joke?

"If you're not, do you think your mother would mind?"

Mr. Boyal's smile folded away. "I'll tell her you might call one day."

"You couldn't suggest me to Ben, could you, Mr. Boyal? Let him know I'm available for work?"

Mr. Boyal paused. "I don't think that would be a good idea." He continued, "It's not you; it's him. He's too independent." And finally, in only a whisper, "Chuck, trust me. Forget about Ben."

Chuck Paa walked home. It was Saturday night, and he drew his bath and plugged the television into the outlet by the mounted toothbrush holder. There was a made-for-TV movie on about a surgeon who was the only doctor in California who knew how to perform microscopic surgery on a rare heart condition called Chunt's disease. In the second part of the movie the doctor's wife came down with the disease herself, and the rest of the movie—as Chuck guessed—was about the doctor preparing to cut up and sew back together his wife's heart. Soaking, Chuck wondered if he could have ever made a fine doctor. Dr. Paa, the cardiologist. Dr. Paa, the dermatologist. A vision of a grateful patient rose before him, her skin cleared and rid of a hideous weeping rash. That's the type of doctor he would have become, transforming a marked face with a pill and a scrub.

Chuck stepped into his white jeans and pulled on a gray sweatshirt that read MAINE. Combing his hair in the mirror, he saw the patch of stubble on his cheek and scraped a dry razor over it. He saw the scars—along his jaw, on the forehead, on the butt of his chin. He was on his way to Chaps, the disco in the Back Bay where two years ago on a night not unlike tonight he had met a stranger with pale blond hair. After shaking hands the two had danced together, Chuck's hips rotating wildly. The black walls and carpet and the cigarette smoke and smoldering dry ice made the place so shadowy that it was only after the stranger, Ben, invited Chuck home, laying a hand on his nape, that Chuck realized that Ben was Bennett, Bennett Wriston, Bennett of *Bennett Boy*. Once they were in front of the disco, beneath the yellow street lamp, Chuck assumed Bennett would recognize him as well, would cup Chuck's face between his hands, but Bennett did not. Surely the china-jar lamps of a well-appointed apartment on Dartmouth Street would reveal things as they were, but Bennett never bothered to turn on the lights when they got to his place. And all night Chuck lay in the wide bed with the goose-down pillows, anticipating the angle of morning light that would finally inform Bennett of their good fortune, and then Chuck could stop calling Bennett "Ben," as he'd been doing all night. But in the morning Bennett looked sad, his mouth hanging at the corners, and he refused to look Chuck in the eyes. When Chuck asked Bennett for his phone number, he stopped, looked around as if startled, and then wrote out the number so slowly that Chuck wondered if Bennett was having trouble with his memory. Chuck asked, "When can I see you again, Ben?" but the only answer to appear was: "Um, I'm not really sure."

Examining his egg-shaped face in the mirror, Chuck hoped tonight he would meet someone like Eugene, the truck driver. And then Chuck Paa had this idea: Oh, how orderly and understandable life would be if everybody always wore his job's uniform with his first name stitched to the pocket.

Except: What would Chuck wear?

———

"That's the best news I've had all day." Mr. Riley sat in his office, his fists on his desk.

Chuck stirred the coffee in his Styrofoam cup. "I thought you'd be happy." He bared his teeth; the job would provide insurance as well, and Chuck could take his teeth for a polish.

"Guess what this means," said Mr. Riley.

Chuck had no idea; he sat in his chair, one eye toward the window in Mr. Riley's office that surveyed the warehouse. Where was Eugene? What was it that Mr. Riley actually believed Chuck could do for him? Mr. Riley, with his shag of black hair and the hooded eyes and the gold dolphin pendant around his throat that had once belonged to Harold. Mr. Riley, his fingers filthy with ink and cut up by bottle caps. You'd have to look hard at him to see any resemblance to sweet dead Harold, master of two tabby cats.

"This means you'll be getting a Jeep," Mr. Riley said. "You know how to drive, don't you, Paa?"

When he tried to explain it to himself, Chuck had moved away from Maine because he was afraid of the people he knew. Too many snarls, too many mouths twisted in distaste. Yet in the South End most of the men, at least the healthy ones, terrified him just the same. They growled like the pack of boys in high school who had called him Chuck Paw, the Animal. And whenever he ran into Ben, Ben's face would tighten with pallid rejection. *It's like there's something wrong with him,* Chuck overheard Ben screech to a bar buddy one night from behind a mirrored pillar at Chaps.

"Hey, Paa."

"Yes, Mr. Riley?"

"You do know how to drive, don't you?"

"I can learn."

"You'd better, because I'm going to give you one of my Jeeps so you can carry the samples with you. How does that sound?"

"A Jeep?" Chuck said. As long as Mr. Riley left him alone, he knew he'd be okay.

"I've got twenty-four brands of beer from places like Iceland, Malta, and South Korea. I want you to make the gays love them." He jabbed his finger into Chuck's soft breast. "You can do that for me, can't you?"

"Sure," Chuck said. "I sure can."

Mr. Riley had poked Chuck where a large pit of a pimple was growing. It was the size of a cherry, a hard core on his sternum, and Chuck had come to call it his crab apple. He didn't know why. It was smaller than a crab apple, but its red soreness, the scar he knew it would leave, reminded him of the welts that had bloomed on his skin after the eleventh-grade field trip to the beach when his classmates pelted him with a sack of stony crab apples. Forced to seek refuge in the icy waves, Chuck bobbed in the ocean as he watched his skin turn blue. When the boys had thrown the last crab apple, he emerged from the sea shaking and wrinkled. Once home, he locked the door to the bathroom and examined his skin for hours, fascinated by the bruises that had erupted like ripe fruit.

"You guys love," Mr. Riley was saying, "anything trendy and imported. We've got to make these beers chic. I've got a marketing gal helping me with that. You just need to take her message to all the bar owners in New England."

Chuck nodded.

"Old Harry was the worst," Mr. Riley continued. "He'd buy into any fad. That's the type of customer we're going for here." He tapped a pencil's grimy pink eraser against a stack of *Beer Business* magazines. He plucked a red thread from the fur of his arm. "Think of Old Harry."

Harold Riley and Chuck Paa hadn't talked much during the five months they worked together. Harold was a broad-chested man with blue eyes and hands as large as Chuck's face. Typically, during the days when Chuck was with him, Harold read novels written by women. Occasionally they spoke, for the most part about items Harold needed at the Star Market or a new treatment he'd been selected to participate in or about a trip to California he hoped to make, to visit his first love, also dying, who lived in a bungalow overlooking the Rose Bowl. Once Chuck had suggested that maybe Harold wanted somebody else to work for him, or maybe he didn't need anybody at all, and Harold had said, his voice all balm, "Don't be ridiculous."

If it had been fifteen years earlier and all the dying men were healthy and playing volleyball, he'd probably have become a waiter, Chuck thought. Why not? Feeding people is important, though nobody thinks of it that way, nobody gives it that kind of respect. Maybe he'd have worked in a hotel restaurant where at least he'd get to wear a tuxedo. But a tuxedo probably wouldn't fit him well. And what about fifteen years from now, or even five? What about in fifteen months? Would all this be over? All these men, skeletons in their robes, returned to the streets, with a cocktail of a cure flowing in their blood? After all the deaths he'd seen, after the daily tally on the *Globe*'s obit page, it was hard to imagine the nightmare ending, but Chuck had to look out for himself. What would he do if he found himself out of a job?

"Do you think I'll have any trouble with the Jeep?" Chuck asked Mr. Riley.

"You'll get used to it in no time. You'll get the whole job in no time at all. You'll be fine, Paa."

But if a tuxedo wouldn't fit him well, what would? Sometimes Chuck wished his mind would stop, that the inexhaustible worry about his future well-being would cease for a moment. A rat on its wheel inside his head: That was how he thought of it, and the rat never rested; Chuck never ceased to fret over how he'd pay for his next meal. He'd gone hungry in Maine, gone to bed with powdered milk and dried potatoes lurching in his stomach. You only have to go hungry one night to spend the rest of your life afraid of a pang in the gut. But sometimes Chuck wished he could quiet the fear. In his head, day after day, he heard the joints of the silver wheel turning, a trill in his skull. . . . If it had been fifteen years earlier, he of course wouldn't have known to sleep safely with men—which with Ben that one and only time he had failed to do—and now he'd need to hire someone like himself to help him die. Last week, after leaving Mr. Boyal, Chuck finally returned to the free clinic to hear the results of his test. He didn't like sitting in the plastic bucket seats of the reception area with the skull-faced men, waiting to be called. Typically he worked for these men. Now he was one of them, or almost: He *could* be one of them. *There's* something new, Chuck thought. Never before had he felt that way about any group: that the right to membership lay like a puppy in his lap. When the social worker with the bobbed hair scooted him into her office and told him he was negative, he didn't know what to say. "How do you feel?" she had asked. "Got that little urge to change a few bad habits?" But Chuck Paa couldn't answer. He stared at her pie-shaped face, reaching for his parka and backing away. And just before he slipped through the door and down the hall, he remembered to ask, "Are you sure?" And then, "You're absolutely sure?"

"What should I wear when I call on the customers?" Chuck asked Mr. Riley.

"You'd know more about that than me, Chuck. Wear whatever you'd wear to a gay bar."

"I'd wear this."

"You'd wear that?"

"Yes."

"Then wear it and see how it goes. But maybe clean up your sneakers." Mr. Riley grinned. His teeth could stand a polish as well. "Keep the shoes clean and business will be good. That's my motto. Hey, look at me."

But Chuck couldn't look at Mr. Riley; Chuck had yet to consider how all this might change the daily throb of his life.

"Let's see you in here on Monday, then," Mr. Riley said.

"Monday," Chuck repeated, and the two men shook on it.

"And put some force into that grip of yours," said Mr. Riley. "Nobody likes a dead fish in his hand."

On the train home, Chuck sat in the sun. The cups of coffee had left him queasy, the grit of Cremora on his teeth. His jiggling leg sent the man next to him, who was clutching a newspaper, to a seat further down the aisle. Driving the Jeep up and down New England, Chuck would no longer run into Ben. The heart of the job, Chuck supposed, would be the solitary hours cruising a highway, his Jeep loaded with beer. That would be fine with him. Plenty of time for thinking and sitting alone. He'd have to phone his contacts, the ones who'd been so good about sending work his way, letting them know he was no longer in the business of helping others; *I'm leaving the dying industry—before it leaves me.* They'd protest his decision, doubting his motives. *If it's about money,* one might offer, but Chuck would return the receiver to its cradle if they droned on too long. *I have to go,* he'd say. He had bars to drop in on, and the hot iron waited for his khakis, and his sneakers needed a roll in the wash.

The sun massaged open his pores, probing deep, warming his eyelids, and Chuck Paa settled inside, recalling, remotely, his evening baths with Bennett. The hours in the Jeep would be like this, too. The rush of the road, the pop song on the radio, the angle of sun in its daily arc. He'd discover his favorite gas stations along the way where they sold hot coffee and sugar cookies, where an attendant in coveralls worked the pump, smeared with grease. Through the days, along the road, from Connecticut to Maine and over to Vermont and out, several times in a season, to Provincetown, Chuck would listen to his thoughts and fiddle with the radio, adjusting the reception, and in some ways he would have successfully removed himself from the cruel pulse of the world. It was better this way; better for him to be alone; the ones he loved, the ones who didn't mind his habits and his ways, were dead and dying, and this left Chuck neither sad nor engulfed with loneliness. No, he took comfort in the inevitability. He took comfort in the check Mr. Riley had given him as a signing bonus: $100, scratched with Mr. Riley's illegible signature.

The train rattled toward Boston, toward the city awash in pink dusk, the car not empty but hardly full, a couple of girls in plaid Catholic school skirts, the man who had slid away from Chuck reading the *Herald*, a grandmotherly type with a sack of knitting, a kid swallowed by his Red Sox cap. The check was in the pocket of his parka, and Chuck brought it out to inspect again. Was it really his? And there'd be more?

But folded with the green check was a scrap of paper Chuck didn't recognize. A note to himself? But Chuck didn't write notes to himself. A list of some sort, but Chuck didn't make lists. He unfolded it, and saw it wasn't his but Mr. Boyal's final grocery list, from the last day he worked for him: more sugar cookies, a can of pickled beets, two filets of marinated perch. Dropped in the parka pocket and forgotten forever, retrieved with the check from Riley WorldWide Inc. Could Mr. Boyal be on some sort of recovery? Who would inform Chuck Paa when Mr. Boyal died? Chuck held the bonus check and looked to his future: the jukebox bars and the discos with the blacked-out windows and the security guard in the parking lot, where Chuck would sell his beers; the median strip of the highways he'd come to know. So much to look forward to, that and the jagged, almost hostile signature of Mr. Riley on Chuck's biweekly paycheck; and the steadiness of a job with a Jeep and a stack of business cards with his name printed out, Chuck Paa, Sales Associate. Chuck Paa, Vice President of Sales—that was Chuck's mind running ahead of itself again. Chuck Paa, on the cover of *Beer Business* magazine, salesman of the year. It didn't take much for

Chuck to imagine; regret failed to overwhelm him as he returned the grocery list to the pocket of his parka. He felt nothing, nothing but the rush of cold air as the train doors opened and no one entered the car but Eugene.

He wasn't wearing coveralls but instead slacks pressed with starch, and a cable-knit sweater, his hair combed slickly across his forehead. He had washed his face and scraped away the oil between his fingers, and Eugene looked somehow more real like this, sparkling and tidy and fresh with a lemony scent—or so Chuck guessed that's how he'd smell. They could ride the train together, and maybe stop at a noodle shop for dinner; split a beer at Club Café or the Luxor in Bay Village, swapping alarming memories of their youths. If they spent the evening together, then Chuck would have a friend on the first day of his job; and it all felt as if something were turning for Chuck, the spin of fortune's wheel whirring for the sake of his welfare—the new job, the bonus check, the fine sight of Eugene on the train. Chuck stood and waved; he parted his lips to call out to his new colleague, his new comrade. Would it be too much to think of him as his new pal, Eugene?

But Eugene didn't see Chuck; he was asking the woman with the knitting what stop should he get off at if he was going to the South End. How many more stops was it? Chuck whispered, "Eugene. Eugene, I'm over here." But Eugene failed to recognize Chuck; Eugene looked Chuck's way and saw no one at all.

Eventually Chuck gave up, and his hand returned to picking the rim of his face. Maybe the job wouldn't turn out as he hoped; maybe Eugene had seen through him, as if he were skinless and not really there. The train stopped again, the doors opened, a burst of cold evening air, and Eugene folded his arms across his chest and shivered, and Chuck understood that in Eugene's eyes he didn't exist. Eugene wasn't expecting Chuck Monday morning; Mr. Riley hadn't told Eugene anything at all. The final grocery list fell from his parka pocket to the floor of the train and the wind hurrying through the open door carried it away from Chuck Paa, and he lunged for it, missing, whimpering about it being Mr. Boyal's last: the final item on the list said this: *Coconut doughnuts!—I'm feeling good enough to eat junk food again!* And the cold breeze returned as the doors began to close, taking the green bonus check too, snatching it from Chuck's moist fingers and hurling it at the floor, down the aisle of the train, and then the doors were closed and Chuck sat stunned, his hands empty, but the car remained chilly and just then an icy feeling of remorse passed through Chuck Paa, like a frigid wave on a Maine beach, surging between his legs and through his groin, shocking his genitals into retreat, and passing before he could let out a cry.

THE DRESS

It was summer and I was ten. My father said they'd be gone for two hours, out pricing a washing machine. "Watch the castle for us, King." His arms were spilling appliance brochures and his stockinged ankles were peeking from his trousers. "We're taking Grandpa along." In the front hall, where my father's cardigans hung heavily on the coat tree, my grandfather waited, white hair greased over the crown of his head, chin soft where it met the throat, eyes a pale, almost feline blue. There was nothing I hated more than when the world commented how much the three of us looked alike. Then Mother scooted both of them out the door.

My sisters were on their way to Marian Minnihan's, whose parents had recently dug a pool into the chaparral hillside of their yard. The pool's redwood deck hung like a balcony over the arroyo, Debbie had reported, impressed. "That's because the Minnihans are rich," Debbie said, her arms freckled and folded across her chest. "Yes, but do they have a dumbwaiter?" my father countered proudly, as if ours had ever worked. "Do they have a separate floor for the servants?" he said, as if anyone had ever occupied the empty rooms at the top of our house.

Our driveway was on a slope and hooked like a backward *S*, curving alongside a hedge of pink oleander whose poisonous properties Dottie would point out every time we climbed into the car. From the window in the upstairs hall, from behind the orange Roman shade, I watched my father back his putty-colored car down the drive. The car slowly rolled onto the burned-out lawn, chewing a patch of dirt, and I could see my mother in the passenger seat look up from the hole of her purse and cheerfully tell my father he was on the grass. "I know that, dear," his lips mouthed. And in the backseat, my grandfather, fussing with the knot of his tie.

My sisters followed, down the drive in swimsuits with towels borrowed—as my mother put it—from the motel across the street from the Hotel del Coronado, a motor inn with pitted-aluminum patio furniture where we stayed on our family vacation, six of us in the Aloha Vista room. The girls wrapped the towels around their waists and turbaned their heads so that a tail of towel fluttered down their backs, advertising CASA DEL CORONADO MOTEL AND FILLING STATION. Their plastic high-heel sandals, bought in Tijuana for twenty-five cents, clacked against the concrete like the silver bells that fell from the eucalyptus. Their chatter—about Marian Minnihan's new haircut, about her mother's white mink coat, about her brother Rex, who one day, all three agreed, would make a handsome boy—mixed with the afternoon call of the blue jays.

Then they were gone.

The house was both big and hot. A widow, Mrs. Trunke, died there during a September heat wave, forty years to the day after her husband built it for her on a hill dense with pepper trees back in 1912. When I was seven my dreamy, awkward-limbed father bought it from Mrs. Trunke's estate, unable to fathom why such a crumbling hulk of a house—brick nibbled at by creeping ficus, mortar shaken loose by earthquake, twenty rooms empty and echoing a bygone era—would remain unsold. "It's perfect," I'll always recall my father saying on our first day in the house, his arms spread and his bony white wrists betraying his lack of handyman skills. "We'll turn it into our perfect house."

But after three years my father had made almost no improvements. Mrs. Trunke's lilac-and-trellis wallpaper, water-stained and peeling, still hung in the TV room, a former sitting room that my father's latest debt-burdened acquisition dominated, its rabbit ears pulled to full extension and drooping in search of reception. In the bedrooms the original rose-colored carpets remained, stains of wear ground into the nap. The house's brass doorknobs and keyholes, its lantern lamps and its heating panels, were as black as rot, unpolished in a generation. And there was a third floor, mysterious in its distance from the parts of the house where we lived, with four bedrooms connected by a dark hall, its wood floor sticky with disintegrating varnish. When Mrs. Trunke was a young bride, the top of the house had served as quarters for her household staff. Now there was nothing up there except the original black corrugated rubber mats nailed to the floorboards and, in one room, a circle of metal folding chairs, arranged by my father in an attempt to furnish what he could not afford.

I climbed the back stairs. The third floor had trapped the summer heat, and the air felt as dry as the sumac-gold hills I could see from the little oval-topped window at the top of the stairs. Although once it had scared me—Dorrie claimed that Mrs. Trunke had collapsed to her death up there—I'd learned early that the third floor was the only place in the house where I could sit and read and not hear my sisters' voices rising and rising like engines finding only higher gears.

There was a closet, deep as a little room, with a sloping ceiling and a row of nose-shaped hooks. Hanging on a lead pipe were two canvas garment bags packed with Mrs. Trunke's clothes. Two cedar drawers, swollen in the heat, offered cream kid gloves and lemon satin pumps and even a white ermine stole, its rodent mouth shellacked and hinged as a clasp. Dorrie, Dottie, and Debbie liked to play there, hauling into the room with the metal chairs armfuls of tea gowns. They would dress each other and their many friends, who were often sisters themselves, their six, ten, twelve girlish voices confidently loud. Occasionally I'd quietly slip into the room, timidly joining their laughter and excitement over Mrs. Trunke's outfits, observing the unstated rules of play. I would hold an organdy dress to a sister's chest when it seemed the right time, suggesting a felt bathing-cap hat to match, or the correct yellow-glass butterfly brooch to pin to a lapel, until one of their faces, usually Dottie's, would freeze icy and hard, and she'd say, as if it had just occurred to her, "But you're not a girl." An embarrassed silence would fill the room, until someone, usually one of the friends, would say, "Yeah." And then again, from someone else, "Yeah."

I went to the closet. It was even hotter in there, the air smelling like the red clay of a baseball infield. I pulled from a satin-wrapped hanger a dress I'd seen one of the friends, Marian Minnihan in fact, try on a month or so ago. It was green gingham with eyelet trim and an Empire waist. Its moon-white sash was long and rubber-banded into a fat roll. Marian had tied her waist with it and then crisscrossed it over her chest, delicately denting the cushions of her breasts, knotting an enormous bow at the top of her spine. She had placed her fists on her hips and begun to strut up and down the hallway that connected the rooms, turning every few feet in tight circles, the puppy ears of the bow flopping against her back. Dorrie had said Marian looked dumb, but I was growing wide-eyed, a sweet, dirty *wow!* of a thrill shivering across my skin. "This is what debutantes wear in West Virginia," Marian Minnihan had said knowingly, with such confidence that no one, not even Dottie, dared to suggest she was making it up.

The third floor's empty, dark rooms were perfect for dressing up and dancing, for bustling about, for hurrying from door frame to door frame like a soprano singing her ails. Perfect for playing, except for one thing. There was no mirror. And that was all the fun, seeing the dress twirl, seeing my pale thin arms hug the bodice, tucking my genitals behind my closed thighs and then lifting the skirt to see the blank triangle of my crotch.

I took the dress to my parents' bathroom, the only room in the house with a reliable lock. It was larger than my bedroom and had two pedestal sinks gray with eggshell cracks and a green rubber floor trimmed, all the way around, with a strip of white vinyl. In its day money couldn't buy a fancier bathroom floor, my father told me the day we tried to scour away its stubborn black stains. It reminded me of the squeegee blade I used to wash the house's front windows, shredded and smelly. At the far end of the bathroom hunched my mother's claw-footed tub. Rust scabbed its inside, but when filled the tub looked like a calm, glass-green pond.

I ran the water and then pulled off my clothes. My briefs were dingy gray, the elastic waist saggy. In the mirror I noticed my long legs, a promise, Dr. Gasper had reported, of the height to come in my teens. My legs were smooth, gold from the summer of lurking around the neighborhood with nothing to do, with a solitary freckle on the inside of my left thigh. My nipples were uneven and oblong, and Oh how I hated to reveal them to the sun and the world whenever Rex Minnihan invited me over for a swim. They reminded me of the pennies my father, my grandfather, and I flattened on the train tracks outside the station at the corner of Del Mar and Raymond. He would hunt the gravel for the smashed coins, searching in the night with the patience of a hound, my grandfather aiming the flashlight, while I hung on to the car door, ready to go home, wondering why they bothered to bring me at all, wondering if my father was silently acknowledging that it really didn't matter if I was there or not.

And then I slipped the dress over my head. It didn't fit properly, tight in the chest and reaching only mid-shin, but I chose not to notice the absurdity, the fact that it looked as if I were wearing a pillowcase, or worse. To me, it looked like an elegant gown, and I an elegant if naïve girl. When I thought it—*you look like a girl*—nothing in me shuddered with loathing or fear because I hadn't yet discovered those outgrowths of the self. I rightly knew that I was playing, and that I wasn't; that the impulse to dress up and dance meant nothing, and that it meant something. I loved looking like a girl, although I knew I wasn't one, because it somehow brought to life the vague, ticking-away feeling that I wasn't a boy either, or at least not like the other boys I knew, certainly not like Rex Minnihan, that I was exactly what Marian Minnihan had said when she caught me clasping a purple-bead bracelet around my wrist: "Why, you're not a boy," she stated, neither shocked nor angry. "You're a girl-boy."

My father listened to a shortwave radio on the windowsill while he shaved. When I turned it on, a lady was singing, her voice a twinkle of birdsong. From the bathroom window I could see across the Arroyo Seco to the neighborhood of black oak and cypress trees where the Minnihans lived. I thought I spotted the blue flash of a swimming pool tucked into the hillside, but I wasn't sure if it was theirs; so many were being dug in those days after the war. The lady on the radio suddenly stopped singing and there was silence filled with the sounds of a shifting audience, and a woman coughing. Then another woman began, her silvery voice reminding me of the night earlier in the summer when my father took me, on an outing he called Boys' Night, to the Hollywood Bowl to hear the final scene of an opera called *Siegfried*. When Brünnhilde woke from her slumber, singing her first words, *"Heil dir, Sonne!,"* a blow of terror pressed tenderly against my chest. When the soprano, a tiny Norwegian with red hair, opened her mouth, the silvery peal split me open, the notes dragging tears from my eyes, and I had never before felt more exposed to my father. I was both hurt and shocked that he would bring me to something like this. It almost seemed obscene, the enormous, squared *O* of her mouth yanking from me strings of private emotions, my fragile self splayed out in front of my father like a set of entrails. All the while my father sat happily, swaying slightly, his finger playing the conductor's baton. When I looked at him he turned to greet my stare with his bucktoothed smile, and I cautiously stood from the bench and backed my way out of the row, knocking programs from laps, and then ran to the car, incredulous that people could listen to music like this and ever face one another again.

I went to the mirror at the back of the door and unrolled the sash. I wrapped it around my waist three times, sucking in my little pad of a gut so that it girdled my middle. I'm an hourglass, I thought, admiring my waist, which cinched up to something no bigger than a thigh. But the sash was long, with yards of extra satin and, Oh what would I do with all of it? What did a pretty young girl do with such a long sash? And so I threaded the two ends of the ribbon through a little hole at the back of the dress's bodice, where the zipper seam had frayed. Then I pulled both ends between my legs inside the dress, wrapping the whole thing around my waist underneath the dress. The two ends I wired through the hole again, and then tied a firm knot with a pert bow at the small of my back. I closed my eyes and felt the satin against my thighs, and everywhere else.

The first lady came back on the radio, this time singing something that made me think she was even sadder than before. I twirled myself when her voice lifted and sank to my knees when I was sure she was singing, crying really, about a lost love. In the mirror I watched myself attempt to mouth the words, my small, open lips nowhere near synchronizing with the voice. But I didn't care, for the music and the dress—the freedom to play, to curtsy and to clutch my breast, to arch my eyebrows and press my fingertips to my lips—the rare, uninterrupted moments of an afternoon to pretend and dream provided me with the fun I failed to find on the soccer field, in Rex and Marian Minnihan's swimming pool, or anywhere else. "So what?" I sang in my closest imitation of the lady's voice, which had become a violin-induced trickle, as if she were dying but not dead yet, and just as I shut my eyes and parted my lips to sing a few more notes with the dying lady, just as my throat began to relax and produce my girlish head voice, just when the fleshy globe of the past and future split itself in two, a fist landed on the door and a pip-squeak of a voice called out, "Hey, Reggie, what're you doing in there?"

My eyes snapped open to the suddenly garish sight of myself in the mirror.

"Reggie? You in there?"

"Yeah."

"Hey, Reggie, it's me."

"Who?"

"What do you mean, who? It's Rex. I came over with the girls." On the other side of the door I could picture Rex Minnihan: canvas sneakers, short pants revealing the tea stain of a birthmark on his thigh, tendons leaping from his throat, teeth sinking into his bottom lip, a cowlick up but wilting in the late summer. The swimming pool's chlorine had turned his hair a lemony yellow since the end of school.

"I'm taking a bath," I declared, disoriented and now resentful that my first chance in weeks for private play was barged in on.

"Then get out. I came over to play."

I began to walk in a circle of hurt. I blamed my sisters for betraying me by bringing Rex back to the house, as if they'd known not to leave their little brother alone for even an hour. And so there was nothing to do but dismantle the afternoon. "I'm coming," I called as I began fiddling with the sash. As it turned out, I'd tied the knot tighter than I realized; I shouldn't have knotted the sash where I couldn't see it, I thought, my elbows out as my hands continued fussing behind my back.

"Hey Reggie, what's taking so long?" Rex began to bang on the door, the mirror shaking in its door frame.

"I'll be out in a sec."

"Why don't you just let me in?" The doorknob began to tremble, and my fist jumped to my eyelet neckline and began clawing at it. What was Rex trying to do?

I twisted the sash so that the knot was at my side. Maybe I could wiggle out of this thing. I tried to roll the belts of ribbon down over my ass, but they jammed at my hips and inside the dress. The ribbon pulled between my legs was now bunching up on the tiny white peach of my scrotum. The pressure on my testicles was a deep purply pain, so buried it almost felt like it was happening to someone else. The sinking feeling in my chest was equally remote, as if I knew profoundly that, in spite of the immediate terror of Rex working the doorknob harder and harder, I was not so incompetent that I could get myself inextricably tied up in a green gingham dress. In fact, the thought of it—*But nothing like that would ever happen to one of us!* my father would often cluck—calmed me, and I said, "Rex, go downstairs. I'll be out in five minutes." From nowhere I had pulled the tone of a woman snappily putting the brakes on her kissy man, and my instant resourcefulness gave me enough of a steady head to press my palms flat in the air and think, Now, let's get out of this old thing.

Rex had apparently sulked away. Only silence on the other side of the door. I moved closer to the mirror to inspect myself, lifting the skirt to see the grape-stain impressions the tight sash was leaving on my skin. The dented flesh looked raw, and I began to worry about scarring and about what invention I would have to create to convince my future wife—for even in this predicament it did not occur to me that one day I would love a man—of the pure origins of the bluish tissue slashing my hips and inner thighs. *I was born this way,* I could tell her with a face so stony and impenetrable she would never dare bring up the subject again. Yes, that would be a useful excuse for many things to come, I realized, gracefully held in a still instant of revelation in my parents' bathroom with the green rubber floor, my skirt scooped up in my arms. What on earth could anyone say to such a comment? It would cut off all argument, it would silence my opponents, and just as I was beginning to think I had discovered one of the major maps to my life, a crashing thud landed against the door, stretching it, causing a tremble in the door frame. And then another came. And then another.

"When are you coming out?" Rex barked, his hard little body flinging itself against the door again and again. "What's wrong with you? I came over to see you!"

I stood back, my fingers madly working at the knot. I desperately pulled my arms out of the sleeves and shimmied the bodice down my chest. I began to yank on the skirt, feeling the sash cinch tighter and tighter with each pull. Then a sharp *crack!* eased through the door frame, and the painted wood let out a rifting sigh. As Rex's floppy cowlick appeared from behind the door, I swooped up my tea-length skirt and hopped—feeling like every nineteenth-century heroine on the run I'd ever read about— across the floor and into the claw-footed tub. By the time Rex was in the bathroom, I was standing in the warm water, the wet dress hanging from my waist, limp, sheer, and unerotically sad.

Rex's face, his freckles dark, froze in confusion, as if someone would have to explain this to him later. I smiled pathetically, my hands spread modestly over my crotch. He stood there, his mouth ajar, his left hand trailing delicately back to the doorknob. "Sorry," he muttered, his voice so shaken I knew he wasn't on his way to tell all.

When he was gone I didn't have time to nurse my indignity. I tried to relock the door, but the bolt was hanging like a loose tooth. Wet, the sash's knot was smaller and tighter, and I became so enraged by the broken lock on the door that I began to rip at the dress. I'm not sure why I hadn't thought of this sooner, but probably it was because, even after Rex's visit, I was slow to realize that something—yes, something—had spoiled my play day.

Before long the dress was hanging in strips from the tenacious sash, which now wrapped the small box of my loin. The ribbon was as thin and dingy as a shoelace, its taut lines pressing into my red skin. All the tugging had shimmied the knot down to a few inches above my penis, which I noticed, as one with horror notices a tick on the leg, was hard. It was no longer than a key, and about as shiny. What it was doing I had no idea. My only other erections thus far had come accidentally when I was lying on my stomach on the gold velvet sofa in front of my father's television set watching the man at the desk read the news from the curling papers in his hands, the knuckle-sized lump in my shorts snuggled arousingly into the soft V of the two cushions. And the more I strangled the sash's knot the longer my penis held firm, its tip beginning to ache.

"Everything okay, King?"

At the sound of my father's voice, I dropped the knot and looked at myself in the mirror on the back of the door that separated us, his breathing coming through from the other side.

"Rex said you might need my help?"

It was a question I wished I had years to answer. Did I need his help? Would it be worth it? But I didn't have the luxury of time to weigh every implication of bringing in my father or not. I was still stuck in the remains of a dress and the hard wet sash was beginning to hurt. I *did* need his help, more than ever, and a wave of ill-timed reasoning swelled inside me and I thought to myself, But isn't he still my dad?

I covered myself in his candy-red robe that was hanging on a hook by the shower. The robe was like a dress itself, or an outer-coat, with a matching sash hanging in belt loops. It was too big for me, and my hands got lost in the sleeves. When I opened the door and emerged, my father, his hands in his pockets and his heels rocking, simply said, "All clean, Kingaroo?"

I walked into my parents' bedroom. The bed was made with a blue blanket with an aqua satin binding. I sat down on the edge. With his lips pursed he shrugged his shoulders and lifted his eyebrows. "Reggie, you're forgetting we're co-pilots. If something's eating at you, then tell me. What's the secret pass-word?"

"Bess," I mumbled.

"Bess what?"

"Bess Truman."

"Bess Truman it is!" He clapped his hands and then prod-ded, "Kingaroo?"

"Yes?"

"What's wrong?"

"Nothing."

"Nothing what?"

"Nothing, Prince Dad." With that, again I felt the grip of the sash. My father remained standing in front of me, only closer now, my eyes looking into his stomach, the small sag of which tested the buttons of his cardigan. My parents' bedroom smelled like carpet shampoo and the powder my mother dusted herself with. Panes of afternoon sun spread themselves across the rug

and a blue jay dashed up and down the eucalyptus branch outside and I held my breath as a wave of shame swept through me
and then moved out. "I can't get out of it," I finally said, loosen-
ing the robe's belt and slowly peeling back its shoulders.

My father's face stopped in time. "King?" he said, his voice a
whisper's sigh.

"The knot's too tight." And we both looked at the wet shreds
of dress and the grimy fist of the sash, like a grotesque outie
belly button. But even more startling than that was my sturdy
little erection, persistently defiant and appalling, just below.

Suddenly, as if someone had snapped his fingers in his face,
my father said, "Everyone's downstairs. Let me get the door."
He began rubbing his hands together as he often did before beginning a project. "We'll have you out in no time," he said, pac-
ing, his eyes aimed at the floor.

With my elbows propping me up, I sat on the bed, my chest
pushed out and my legs spread. I was beginning to shed my em-
barrassment, as if the cloying sash had also numbed any sensible reaction to such exposure. I simply wanted him to get on
with it, to break through the knot I could not, and when he at
last crouched between my thighs, his huge hands delicately
avoiding the red tip of my penis, I realized that the reason I
could no longer feel my shame was because it, all of it, had
transferred to my father, where it sat in blotches in his broken-
heart face. At first I thought he would ask me how this had happened, but then, as his fingers picked hopelessly at the knot, I
saw that he wasn't going to be able to bear the details. He already knew more than a father should.

"I was just playing, Prince," I ventured. He didn't say anything, his head bent in a painful mixture of concentration and confusion. He had thick hair with wiry strands of gray sprouting from the crown, and I felt the regrettable urge to reach out and stroke it. When he felt my hand on his neck, he looked up from his toil, his eyes drooping and watery. It was then I knew what he thought of me, what he would always think of me, how the green gingham dress would be as closely associated with me as the color of my eyes or my love of music, and that even decades from now he would view me from the corner of his eye and wonder how his seemingly upright son was spending his dark, private, incomprehensibly perverse hours.

Oh, I couldn't stand it. I flopped back on the bed and shut my eyes. It was there that I lay for another few minutes that crept by like hours. It was there that I felt my father's hand graze the pipe of my penis and listened to him mutter a terse, angry "Sorry." My father nudged my legs open wider for more work space, and at that my eyes rolled back into my head and I silently begged for a future without the dress. I would do anything to be rid of this whole day, I told myself. Anything to get off the bed. And when my father rather belatedly said, "I'm just going to cut this damn thing," I swelled up with relief, thinking that at last it was over, at last I could sit up and leave his bedroom. He snapped a pair of scissors through the sash, saying, "We'll just have to forget about this." I was at last free, and I put on his robe again and nodded with eager agreement as I left the room, certain that forgetting was a realistic option. For I was ten and my father was a man who whistled cheerfully when he backed his car onto the lawn; we were both built of happy hope. We were both fond of saying, "What difference does it make?" There was no reason to think that I would be lying on my parents' bed in a ripped dress with my father between my legs for the rest of my life. There was no reason to believe the humiliation would last any longer than the sash's red weltish marks. It was over. The welts were in retreat.

But an hour later, when I was dressed and downstairs and saw my father across the kitchen counter, he and I both knew where we were. I was back on the bed. And during the next week, when I passed him in the hall, he would look at me, his mouth twisted as if he didn't know what to say, and I would be sent back to the bed, to my position with my legs spread wide, heavy with the growing feeling it was the only place I belonged. And when, the following Saturday, he found me on the third floor thumbing through Mrs. Trunke's closet, searching for an ivory silk shift Dorrie and Marian Minnihan had sent me to find, he simply said, "Reggie, please," and simultaneously we shuddered, the two of us bereftly aware that our relationship had decayed to the few minutes on his bed. "When are you going to stop this?" he begged, moving away. And I couldn't blame him, for neither of us could withstand the untying of a second knot on a dress. We were counting on the months to pass quickly to lessen the bind of a harshly clear memory, pleading for time to pick up the pace of its slow, ineffective healing. But every morning his blank face over the breakfast bowl continued to send me to the bed. His turned back as we changed in the swimming pool's locker room flung me to the blue blanket. His careful knock before entering my bedroom told me where in his mind I still lay, and how even years later, when searching for a pen dropped beneath his bed, my father would find a stray shred of green gingham; beneath the mattress there'd be a cut of eyelet trim; in Mrs. Trunke's closet he'd find the satin-wrapped hanger on the lead pipe, empty and somehow waiting for the return of its checked dress; and in my face he'd see the real flicker of a son who no longer belonged to him.

THE CHARM BRACELET

It was the middle of the night and Billy Henderson, eighteen and green-eyed and track-star thin, was cutting through the park, in no hurry to get home. The park was officially closed, dark and asleep in its own damp as it waited for dawn. But Billy wasn't thinking about dawn. He was thinking about the evening he'd passed at Club Café, about the phone numbers wadded in his pocket, about the stranger's lips wet on his cheek, when suddenly a twig snapped in the rhododendron ahead and something ghostly rustled among the leaves.

Billy stopped and peered down the path.

Nothing stirred. The rhododendron stood silent.

Then a second branch snapped and Billy felt his throat tighten, but soon the night fell silent again. The wind died and not a leaf in the park swayed, the dogwood blossoms quiet on the branch. And so he told himself to ignore the noise and continue on his way.

He wasn't frightened, not tonight. There was something different about tonight: the yellow moon heavy with glow, the obscene scent of spring loitering in the hyacinth beds, the fleck of knowledge, to which Billy clutched as if it were a house key, that his life, his new life, had begun tonight.

"You're the most beautiful boy in the bar," one man, a doctor on the staff of Harvard Medical School, had said at Club Café. Billy had accepted the doctor's card with the VE RI TAS in raised crimson letters; the card, the compliment, and a sweating rum and Coke. He said he'd call the doctor sometime, not really meaning it. Already there was the card of a TWA pilot in the breast pocket of Billy's yellow checked shirt, an Easter gift from his mother. And penned on a napkin the e-mail address of a logging company executive from Maine. And there was the phone number of the man with no eyebrows, Roger; he was . . . well, Billy never found out what he did for a living because as soon as Billy began sipping the drink Roger sent over, Billy realized there was something wrong with him—there's no other way to put it. The missing eyebrows; the raw picked-at skin; his hands soft, as if boneless; his habit of ending his sentences with *makes you think, doesn't it?*; the way he suddenly cupped Billy's head in his soft boneless hands and kissed Billy's cheek with a wet mouth smacking like the damp twigs breaking in the rhododendron just now.

But as soon as Billy looked up to investigate, the noise in the bush stopped again.

He looked at his watch: pearly face, Roman numerals, an hour hand like a tiny dagger; FedExed last Christmas from his fat-cat dad. The watch's bracelet slid—slinked, really—over Billy's wrist, the links bright beneath the moon, and he held out his hand—like a bride admiring her engagement ring—and delighted in the way the gold fell across his flesh. A narrow wrist, a bump of bone, and a silkiness of skin that Billy knew someday would work to his advantage. And it was only then that Billy noticed the time.

He had missed his curfew by more than an hour, and to make things worse the watch had been running slow lately; so what time was it, after all? Last month his mother had pushed back the time he was due home, but never before had he stayed out this late. She'd let him have it, that's for sure, but Billy wasn't going to worry. Not tonight, when something had given him that first taste of freedom—as if it'd been the most liberating thing he'd ever done, telling his mother he was going to a party at Jonathan Scudder's while instead stepping into the dim pink lights of Club Café, his fake ID burning in his back pocket. Oh, how easy it was to lie to his mother, to trick her into believing any old thing that couldn't possibly be true. It reminded him of the time when he was little and she had asked him if his father had ever touched him *down there*. This was right after Billy's father abandoned them for California to build a fortune on the Internet. Thinking he might gain from it, Billy had answered, "Sort of," although it wasn't true. But it might as well be true,

Billy had thought often. Yes, so many things in life, in Billy's life, might as well be true.

Now from the rhododendron floated a strange scratching noise, almost like a fingernail brushing a piece of nylon. As Billy approached the bushes, the noise padded on, as if it were traveling ten paces ahead. A low fence and cabled wire had trained the rhododendron to grow in a long hedge in the corner of the park, and Billy wondered what would happen when he reached its end. He shoved his hand in his pocket, his thumb rubbing the raised waxy letters of the doctor's card. He thought about turning around, but Billy told himself there wasn't a thing in the world that could scare him enough to alter his course.

And yet, more often than not, Billy felt as if soon he would have to change something in his life. Those men tonight had proven—how should Billy put this?—his potential. An indication of what lolled ahead. His current life in the narrow brownstone with his dieting mother and his debutante sister restricted his every move: who he could meet up with in Harvard Square and what magazines he could read and what Web sites he could visit and even the clothes he could wear, because only yesterday he'd bought with his birthday money a pale denim jacket in a basement shop on Newbury Street and both his mother, with her deep-set eyes, and Nina, with her full scornful mouth, had said the jacket was tacky. *It makes you look cheap;* and Billy found himself both hurt and excited by the comment, wondering if *cheap* was a stand-in for another word. He'd have to continue living like this all summer, three and a half more months to be precise, until at last he could fly out with his new bedsheets and his set of tank tops to the art college in Pasadena, where Billy knew he would explode; where, more likely than not, he'd pierce one or two flaps of skin with a silver hoop of some sort and sink the tattooer's needle into his inner thigh. The problem was Billy was ready to explode *right now;* he thought of himself as an angry red party balloon blown so tightly that electricity skittered across his skin. This was why Billy had skipped Jonathan Scudder's two-kegger and wandered into Club Café, his face scarlet and taut. Now Billy's moist hand clenched the phone numbers of not one but four men who could help Billy escape his hopeless, cramped life—or so each had promised in his own tented-trousers way.

All was calm in the park; the rustling had ceased again, though Billy hadn't noticed when. For the first time, he looked over his shoulder. Nothing. And nothing ahead, nothing in the park but a hedge and a gravel path and a burned-out lamp and a trash bin with a gooey ice-cream dish on its rim, and he was no longer certain where the noise had risen from or if it had risen at all. Billy continued walking, his eyelids heavy and his head spinning with the evening's flattery and the cocktails. He couldn't recall the last time he'd drunk so much, naïvely chasing his beers with rum and Cokes, a martini, and, oh yes, a Manhattan—who had bought him the Manhattan with the skewered cherry as red and glistening as a hen's heart? Instantly the Manhattan had given him a blurry rush. But Billy didn't think he was drunk, or not very. No, it was the excitement of the night and the late hour; the watch reminded him that dawn wasn't far off, and Billy worried that perhaps he had damaged it by wearing it swimming last week. Or had his father sent along the watch knowing it couldn't keep the time? As if it were a prank of some sort—but why would his father do that, treat him like that? They no longer spoke, his father and

Billy; he'd said good-bye to Billy for good, but Billy didn't miss him, self-trained in the art of missing no one. The resemblance was faint; young wiry Billy, perpetually flushed in the cheek, and his father, dark-faced, wrapped in a coat of muscular fat. When he was seven or eight, Billy had once said to him, "Maybe you're not really my dad after all." Where on earth do you get such ideas, Billy? That was his mother, her hand boxing his ear. *Where did he get such ideas?* From his brain, of course; that was his answer to his mother, and that's what he was thinking now, his mind turning out notions, nasty and true, at a pace faster than the world he was born into could absorb. He perceived everything, or so he thought, as if he wore a miner's hat, torchlit; sometimes he pictured himself walking through the city beneath a hard hat, a beam of light surveying what sprawled ahead, nudging the dark, and that was what enabled him to scan the park in the middle of the night and know that danger waited neither ahead nor behind. Why, that rattling in the rhododendron, that was nothing at all; under closer inspection Billy could see the veins in the olive-green leaves, the black iron fence pickets like cupid's arrows holding up the shrub, the spindly branches inside the shrub, where nothing lingered but a white cat shaking out its fur.

All that and only a cat!

And so Billy relaxed with a sense of rescue, as if he'd been teetering on a ledge and the cat had plucked him from a terrible fall.

He exited the park and crossed the street, the house only ten minutes away. Frightened, he had crushed the doctor's card into a hard white ball, and Billy Henderson let out a tiny laugh—a chuckle that sounded, even to him, like the flirty giggle of a careless girl.

"You haven't seen a bracelet, have you?" a voice asked.

Billy turned around. "What?" And then, "Where'd you come from?"

"Back there," the woman said, touching the tight curls of her hair. "You walked right by me."

"I did?"

"Zipped right by. You must've been lost in your own head, kiddo, 'cause you were talking to yourself. Anyways, did you see a bracelet in there along the path? Me, I'm too scared to go back in the park. Being alone and all." She was panting as if she'd been jogging, and there was something slightly askew about her hair, a few frizzy strands moist round the rim of her face.

"A bracelet?"

"I was walking this way earlier, not all that long ago, and then I realized it was gone."

"What was gone?"

"My charm bracelet." She was thin in a skimpy sort of way, dressed in a purple leather skirt, scratched and chipped, and an angora tank top that clung to her rib cage. Tall, too, perched in thong sandals with a gold heel—how had she managed to run in those?—and a purse in the shape of a clam looped over her shoulder on a silky string. Her ankle turned coyly as she spoke.

"You think you lost it in the park?"

"Or on the sidewalk along here. And I've gotta find it. I'll be in deep shit if I don't find it. You sure you didn't see it?"

"What does it look like?"

"Gold, with stars and a moon."

"Real gold?"

"'Course it's real gold," and her arms folded across her

breasts in a way that told Billy she was a woman who expected real gold.

"I didn't see anything."

"You sure?" She said something about knowing this would happen, and she played with the hem of her skirt, which was closer to her crotch than her knee. Out of her mouth came a disgusted sigh: "Oh, he's going to kill me."

"How'd you lose it?"

"I don't know. It's on my wrist one minute and then it's gone. How does anyone lose anything? It's there and then it isn't. I was in a hurry, running and not paying attention."

"Running?"

"Never you mind, kiddo." She said this in a way that indicated she no longer wanted to talk to Billy, but she spread her feet apart and planted herself even more firmly on the street corner; she looked into the park, and then the other direction down the street, and her face—a youngish face, but not too young—pouted in indecision. She mumbled something: might as well have been "What to do?"

"I can help you look for it."

"You're not trying to steal it, are you?"

"Who, me? No, but I'll help you look for it."

She thought about this. "You'd do that?"

"Sure, I'm not in any hurry." He added, for no particular reason: "I have no place to go."

"Oh, so you're one of those kids? Hitched to the street?" She continued eyeing the gate of the park with a vague fear flickering in her eyelid.

One of what kids? But Billy thought he understood, and it

was so late and his head was so awash in drink and flirt that he decided not to correct the woman, or, rather, it felt as though his mouth couldn't form the words of truth about what type of kid he was. Alas, but what did Billy care?

The woman fished a cigarette out of her purse. It bobbed between her lips as she waited for a light from Billy, who was digging through his pocket, bringing up nothing but the business cards and the napkins. "I don't smoke," he admitted.

"Ah, Christ." Her eyes, brown, caked on the lid with blue, rolled in her head, and she handed a matchbook to Billy, who had to strike two or three times before catching a flame. As he brought it to the woman's face he saw more of her: a fine nose, not too fleshy; a high forehead yet to buckle with worry; a fading dark half-moon beneath her right eye. Was that a bruise or a bag from lack of sleep? Hard to tell, but even so everything about her face was symmetrical and lined up; pretty, though probably not for much longer. She smiled, licking her lips, and a hot, pickled breath reached Billy's nose. In the matchlight he could see the bleariness in her eyes, the whites threaded with blood, the moist droop at the corners. The woman is tanked, Billy was thinking, blotto, riding the highest of high horses, but then, suddenly, he feared that perhaps he'd said this aloud. Were his thoughts spewing from his mouth like a yellow foam?

"What's your name, anyway?"

"Billy."

"Nice to meet you, Billy. I'm Mrs. Regina Glume. Formerly Regina Rosemallow." From the clam purse she produced a card that read REGINA GLUME: ACTRESS.

"You're an actress?"

The woman nodded, two plumes of smoke jetting from her nostrils.

"What have you been in?"

"Ever see that commercial for the pancake house?"

"I'm not sure. What about any movies or TV shows?"

Regina bent over, as if the bracelet might be lying at her feet. "I wonder if it's in the park."

"Are you in anything now?"

"There's this part I'm up for." She moved away from Billy, investigating the gutter. Was the bracelet there?

"Do you know anyone famous?" Billy asked.

She straightened herself and placed her fingers on his shoulder: "I know you."

Billy smiled, because sometimes he felt famous, or he imagined himself famous, taking note of the way his foot, perfectly arched and sanded down with pumice stone, fell on the sidewalk or the way his hand took the rail of a staircase, the heavy watch shifting about the wrist, as if his eyes were a news camera recording his every elegant move; and although it wasn't true he somehow knew it would become true one day, people shoving tape recorders beneath his chin and asking him for one more photo. He sometimes wondered what he'd like to be known for: his paintings, oversized and painted in primary colors; or his beauty, delicate, almost feminine but with a brutality at its edge, in the scissor glare of his eye, in the hardness of his breast, in the way the nail on his pinkie tapered sharply—a cruel splendor for which those men tonight seemed prepared to fork over their lives.

Billy tried to return the card but Regina said, "No, keep it. You never know." She shifted her weight from one hip to the other and surprised him by asking, "How about you, little Billy? You out working tonight?"

"Working? Out here? Who, me? Oh no, I mean, no, well, it's not what you think. I'm not what you think—" and then he heard himself say, as if reading a script "—not tonight. I mean, what I'm trying to say is: I'm new at all this."

"You don't look so new at this."

But that wasn't true: Wasn't tonight the first night of Billy's new life? A pit of regret inched up his throat because nothing could happen in his life as long as he lived with his mother and Nina. Billy imagined the intricate deceit he'd have to construct if he wanted to see one of the men from Club Café again. Lying, averting his eyes when he told his mother and Nina, who always lingered in the background like a housefly, that he was headed over to Copley to go to the movies with Edwin Marvin when in fact a man, maybe the logging company executive with the silver eyebrows, was waiting in the lobby of the Ritz, waiting to buy Billy a cocktail with a floating white onion and a pepper-rubbed steak, hoping to take Billy to his room with the yellow brocade curtains where they'd perform on the firm hotel mattress what Billy had never performed in his life. But Billy knew none of this could happen as long as he lived in the dark-halled house where you could hear every footstep; he couldn't even have one of those men phone him, what with Nina's habit of running to answer every call and his mother's annoying way of asking *Who was that?* whenever he returned the receiver to its cradle. But Billy had to do something, he had to tell somebody every last thing that was running through his mind. But who? Maybe he'd call his old man out in Pasadena, not that they'd spoken in two years, not that Billy had received anything from him but a perpetual and generous cash flow and the watch that had arrived unexpectedly last Christmas. His dad had become sort of famous, appearing in *Fortune* and *Wired* and all over the web, and Billy would study those pictures, searching for a trace of himself. Once or twice Billy had picked up the phone and dialed the number and then hung up; "Hello? Hello?" and then Billy had cut the line, words clumped in his throat. What to say to a man who has abandoned you? No, he couldn't call his dad, not now, not at this point; *take the money and run,* he'd heard his mother say, laughing coarsely into the phone while chatting with one of her divorcée friends about who knows what. *I don't give a shit about Dad,* Nina would say at the dinner table, chopping her salad into bits, elbows out, knife *chop chop chop* and Nina's mouth pinched, *Fuck him.* Maybe Billy would invite the Harvard doctor over for dinner, letting his mother *know* with a sly wink at the table as he reached to touch the doctor's scrubbed hairy hand. Imagine that, Billy and the doctor from Harvard Med! Now that would make his mother croak at her own dinner table. But there was something about the doctor that Billy hadn't liked: the way he ran his hand down the knuckles of Billy's spine to his ass, a gesture Billy found more humiliating than exciting. And, anyway, none of this mattered because Billy didn't want to date these old men with their bald spots like upside-down ashtrays, with their huge greedy eyes so much like his father's. No, he loved ripping the power out of their hammy hands, as if to say *I'll show you who's in charge.*

Mrs. Regina Glume took Billy's hand and said, "Should we go into the park to look for it?"

"In there? Now? But it's so late."

"But if it's lying on the path it'll be gone by morning." And then, "You aren't afraid, are you?"

"Afraid of the park? How could I be afraid of the park? Why, I just came out of there; you saw me, didn't you? And besides, I didn't see any old bracelet lying around. If I were you I'd look on the sidewalk, because if it's on the sidewalk it'll be snatched up in a second."

Regina stood motionless, and Billy wondered if she was listening. "Maybe you have a point. So let's go," and she gave his sleeve a tug, taking him in the direction of his house. "Keep your eyes open."

"I always do."

They were walking in step now, Billy scanning the sidewalk but of course there was nothing but leaves pasted to the concrete and a candy-bar wrapper caught in the ivy growing around the base of a tree and the coin of a Rolling Rock cap, dented down the middle. Yet as they made their way down the sidewalk, the night appeared brighter to Billy, as if more of the lantern street lamps had flickered on or the moon had begun to sag closer to the curb. What was he worried about? Why not pretend he was a hustler? Why not go on and make up a story for Regina? Something about it excited him. Sometimes when he shut his eyes and reached into his underpants he dreamed of it: a faceless man crushing him and then leaving a wad of fifties on the nightstand.

"Someone buy you a drink tonight?"

"How'd you know?" said Billy.

"Because a boy like you never buys himself a drink. That comes later. If you're lucky, much later."

"But isn't it nice when they surprise you like that? Sending over a drink and then introducing themselves." Billy recalled the ripple in his chest when the waitress had approached him saying the man across the bar wanted to buy him a Manhattan. Which one is he? Billy had asked. The one in the silk tie?

Regina wasn't paying much attention to the sidewalk, instead deciding that now was the time to tell Billy about herself. And this made Billy think: Yeah, why is she out here in the middle of the night anyway?

"There's no Mr. Glume, not anymore. He was a Canadian and he returned to the North. A contractor. Had a ponytail and a brass belt buckle that said DIRTY DAVE." Was he the one who gave her the charm bracelet? "Who, Dave? Oh, no, he gave me nothing but a messed-up credit report and, if we're going to be honest here, a bout of scabies; that Dave Glume was no good, shouldn't have ever married him. My sister told me the night I met him. Watch out for the Dave Glumes of the world."

"I'll try my best," said Billy.

"Sometimes that's not good enough," Regina warned, although she was hardly speaking to him. "Oscar Rosemallow was just the opposite, so sweet it could make your stomach turn. An assistant at a veterinarian's. Always hiding behind plastic-rimmed eyeglasses and beige turtleneck sweaters. He cooed when he held me, like a filthy pigeon. And smelled like a kennel, but that wasn't his fault—hazard of work. And he was always reminding me of the hazards of my work, trying to get me to stop, not giving me the money to fly to California for an audition. I took a few jobs that maybe I shouldn't have, and old Oscar never forgave me for that."

"What kind of jobs?"

"Oh, you know, Billy. The ones you regret."

So much an actress has to do in life to break in, she said. She sucked on the butt of her cigarette and said something about videos that he couldn't quite make out. "Five hundred bucks sounds like a lot at the time." She flicked the cigarette onto the stoop of a brownstone where a widow lived, Mrs. Christopher Painethrope, who relied on Spanglish to boss around her Portuguese maid. Mrs. Painethrope once asked Billy over to meet a friend of hers, a famous painter from New York who showed little interest in Billy's own artistic ambitions but a great deal of interest in the way Billy's knit shirt fell across his teenage chest. "Call when you come to the city. I'll show you around."

"So, how'd the night go for you?" Regina inquired.

"What do you mean?"

"Much of a payday?"

"Not exactly. I was over at Club Café."

"That the place above the gym?"

Billy nodded.

"Yeah, I hear that's where they go to buy themselves a packet of chicken thighs."

"Chicken thighs?"

"From what I hear, the meat's for sale at that place."

"The meat?" He'd never met anyone like her, and if she frightened Billy he wouldn't admit it to himself. You see, Billy possessed a fundamental understanding of his place in the world; he knew about pecking order, he knew on which rung he stood. The fact of it stayed with him, like his knowledge of the impenetrable copper green of his eyes. "Makes me want to melt you down, those eyes," the pilot had said.

"It was about here that I started running," Regina said. "The bracelet might have fallen off about here."

"Why were you running?"

"I didn't want him to see me."

"Who?"

She was still drunk, Billy realized, but in a giddy sort of way: speaking quickly and with delight in herself, telling him about the time she'd met a producer at a poolside party who asked her to star in a TV movie about the life of Vanna White: "Said he was going to make everyone in America know my name, but then he asked me my name and when I told him he said I'd have to change that right away, there'd never been a star named Regina Glume and there'd never would be. What about Regina Rosemallow? Well, that was better, he said, but not much, and so I left the party with him. I climbed into his rusty DeLorean— 'member those?—but then the movie got red-lighted and so much for that party in Pasadena."

"Pasadena?" said Billy. "That's where I'm moving to. To go to art school."

"Then be sure to stay clear of anyone named Ricky Gold. Nothing but promises and a rusting sports car."

Down the street a tire screeched, and Regina started, jerking her head: "What's that?"

"Just some car."

A banana-yellow Cadillac tore past them, thumping with a beat in its stereo. A panic shimmered in her eyes. "Maybe it's not out here," she said. "Maybe I should give it up and get off the street."

"It's probably still out here somewhere," said Billy. "At this hour there's nobody to pick it up. Come on, we'll find it."

Regina looked around nervously, fingering the V collar of her tank top. They were standing not far from a street lamp, and Billy saw a blot of bruise on the underside of Regina's arm. "You think it's okay?" she said.

"What's to worry about?"

"You're probably right. He has no idea where I am."

Maybe this was what he needed, a special friend like Regina, someone who saw things differently from the rest. Perhaps it'd be cool to tell people he was palling around with a run-down actress, that his best friend had a few videotapes in her past. But it wouldn't be like those stuck-up girls from Cambridge who signed up for community service with homeless people and then told the Friday assembly that they had come to *know* what it was like to live without a roof over their heads. When he'd heard this, Billy had laughed so loudly it echoed in the auditorium, attracting a slit-eyed glare from Señora Vicario, his Spanish teacher. But it was the stupidest thing anyone had said all week, those girls with their four-story houses two blocks from Harvard Yard and their Cambodian maids trying to convince *him* that they knew anything at all. The people in his life were so ridiculous that Billy sometimes thought, yes, he could kill them. Or he might as well kill them. It may sound extreme, but they led lives so far from the one he wanted for himself that sometimes he pointed the gun of his index finger and pulled the trigger of his thumb.

"Are you married now?" Billy thought to ask.

"Not exactly. We're not married or anything. But there's a guy, if that's what you're asking. I'm living with someone. Or was living with someone. I moved out on him last week."

"Why?"

"He turned out not to be as nice as I thought."

Was he the one who gave her the charm bracelet? Yeah, he was the one, somebody named Donny Vickerman, half German, you could see it in the shape of his body, arms like smoked hams. "He started off all nice and everything, buying me all sorts of things, remembering my birthday."

"What sort of things?"

"Bought me a white mink coat with my name stitched inside." In the air her finger spelled out *Regina* in cursive letters.

"How long did you live with him?"

"*Two* years," but her emphasis made it sound more like twenty.

"Where'd you meet him?"

"In a hotel bar."

"Which hotel?"

"The Ritz." She said this proudly.

"I was going to guess that."

A police cruiser sped by, ignoring them, its siren blaring and its light turning everything red for a second. She watched it carefully, with a thought Billy couldn't read in her eyes. Was she holding her breath? Regina took his hand, fingers squeezing uncomfortably on the watchband, and Billy wondered if she was going to drag him into the street and chase after the cops. But why would Regina want to do that?

"Is everything okay?" he asked.

The siren faded, and Regina shook herself out with a shiver. Billy guessed she was a bit older than he had first thought, deep into her thirties; probably the type to lie about her age. His mother was the same way. "Me? Why, I'll be forty next year!"

"What about you?" Regina said. "How'd you end up out here?"

"Like I said, I really am new at this."

"But what got you here?"

"Here?" He looked around: the street at the foot of Beacon Hill caught in the span between dusk and dawn, the town houses with the maids' rooms in the basements, the window boxes planted with late-season tiger tulips, the views from bay windows of the Esplanade and the Charles River, the staircases that led to fifth floors where children played out of earshot from their parents, planning a world war with their dolls, hatching a plot to blow up the family car with yards of string dipped in lighter fluid. "How'd I get here?"

"You know what I mean."

He mentioned a mother who threw him out of the house; he told a story of going hungry, of living off a jar of Hellmann's for three days, of sleeping at the T station, where he traded his first favor for a meal, two jelly doughnuts and a coffee with cream. The fact of it seemed no more true or false than his actual life. He could conjure every detail: the finger in the mayonnaise jar, the odor rising from the pit of his arm, the sugar from the doughnut caking his lip, the terrible heat trapped beneath a stranger's fly. Why did he believe this was true?

But it didn't matter, not to Billy; it all might as well be true.

Regina's face relaxed, her features softening with pity. "It's rough out here. Everything after you, hunting down your ass. You need to find yourself someone and settle down. At least for a few years until you're out of the woods."

It was no different for me, she said. When Regina was his

age, they chased her too; those long legs after a waxing could drive any man crazy; she hitchhiked across the country to California but got herself in some trouble with a casting agent out there. His wife said she'd blow her brains out if she ever saw Regina lurking around their front yard again! "Oh, it was the whole bits," Regina explained. "The crazy wife in a robe and curlers, a French scarf over her head and holding up a little pistol that was so small I was pretty sure it wasn't real but I didn't want to stick around to find out. Not for that loser, the so-called casting agent. Nothing upstairs, and definitely nothing downstairs, and not so many casts to cast, as it turned out. And definitely wasn't as rich as he let on. Took me to a beach house one weekend that turned out to be a shack with a shag rug gone moldy." Regina laughed. "The things we do."

She looked at him; he must have been frowning, with a worry stitched in his face, because she said, "But they're not all like that. Some guys turn out to be all right."

"What about Donny Vickerman?"

"What about him?"

"You think you'll go back to him?"

"Why would I want to do that?"

"I don't know. If he was nice once, maybe he'll be nice again."

"You sure don't know how men work, do you? How they treat you when you meet them is the best you'll get. It's all downhill from there. The trick is to figure out when the slope gets really steep on you."

"Are you sure about that?"

"Everybody knows that. It's a fact. I bet you're the same yourself."

"Me?"

"Well, maybe you're not like the rest of them. I guess we'll have to wait and see about that."

"Wait a minute," Billy said, touching Regina's arm. "What's that?" Ahead of them on the sidewalk lay something small and shiny. They ran to it, but it turned out to be nothing more than a coil of wire.

"Maybe it's lost for good," said Regina. "One more reason for him to kill me."

"He'll probably understand. Tell him the clasp snapped open and it was gone. Just tell him the truth."

"The truth?"

"Or maybe blame it on him. It's his fault for buying you a bracelet with such a weak clasp."

"I doubt he'll see it that way."

"You never know."

"I know."

Regina had released his hand to work free a mint from a foil roll. She offered Billy the last one. The same kind of wintergreen mints his mother sucked on, all day long—a trick to keep herself from snacking. He'd heard the screams, of course, even from the fifth floor of the town house: his mother shrieking as his father had collected his papers, his checkbook, his crocodile-skin jewelry box, "I never fucking loved you, not once, all those times I said it I was lying. *Lying.* Who in her right mind could love *you?*"

Now Billy had lost track of the time; it felt as if he'd been talking to Regina for an hour or longer, as if the gentle pink dawn would rise in the next instant. But no, the moment remained secured in the middle of the night, when nothing budged, the streets waiting empty and dewy, bedrooms warming over with the effluvia of sleep.

"You know what he said when I first met him?"

"Who?"

"Donny." Her eyes slitted up. "Are you listening to me?"

"Yes, of course. What'd he say?"

"He said what they all say but what every girl since the beginning of time believes is true."

"What's that?" Billy felt a pang in his chest, as if he were desperate for this bit of information.

"He said I was the one. And I said, 'I know your type, Donny, and I know you've said that to the other girls, and where are they now?' Donny begged me to believe him, got on his knees, even got teary, and, Billy, believe you me, those are the ones to watch out for, the ones who break your heart on the first night."

Billy wondered if she were giving him accurate advice, because he expected things to work otherwise for him; he had already imagined it: a man, a few years older, handsome in the eye, taking Billy's hand and offering him everything, love and a life. There'd be a house in the foothills of Pasadena and a converted garage with a skylight for Billy to paint in. And a shared bedroom with a terrace facing west, planted with palms. Maybe that doesn't happen to everyone, but why shouldn't it happen to him? Didn't he have the goods?

"So you're all alone now, is that it?" asked Regina. "No family? No one at all?"

"Not exactly." He thought about telling Regina that his father had fondled him when he was younger, but now for some reason the lie sounded profane.

And then Regina did a funny thing: She ran her finger along the vein in Billy's throat, tapping on his pulse. "You need to be careful out here."

Billy had stopped walking. He was looking at her: hair permed out, the soft brown color of his own, hollow of cheek dusted with powder, lipstick bleeding into the cracks around her mouth. He was looking at her but thinking of himself. Sweat was collecting at the small of his back, the cocktails throbbing in his temple, his heart knocking away.

"You aren't working for anyone, are you?" Regina asked.

"Working for someone?"

"You haven't handed yourself over to anyone, have you? That's where the trouble is."

"Oh," Billy said. "Oh, no." He thought of his mother, who'd be asleep with her black silk night mask across her eyes and that sticky ginseng cream she used around her mouth; he thought of how after his father left she had sworn at the dinner table, white wine in hand, that she'd never date another man: Then she wiped a tear with a plastic-red fingernail. How long till that vow was broken? About three weeks.

Billy wondered what her real name was: She wasn't born Regina, nobody's born with a name like that; probably a simple name like Suzy, a skinny girl in frilly white socks and black buckle shoes, but that name and those pigtail days were lost to the world; he knew it as certainly as he knew that when he arrived in California he would dump the name Billy like a dead body and introduce himself as Will.

A horn blared and Billy looked over his shoulder, but the street was empty, the windows of the parked cars glazed with damp. "So, what happened to you tonight? Where are you coming from, anyway?" he asked.

"Me? I was out and about."

"Where are you staying?"

"What do you mean?"

"You said you moved out on Donny. Where have you been sleeping?"

She didn't answer, pulling on the hem of her sweater and impressing Billy with her bony freckled body held up in angora and a little strip of purple leather. He didn't know why, but he felt a kinship to her. It was a crazy thought: Regina and Billy cut from the same cloth? But she reminded him of himself more than anyone he knew. Was it because she had traveled far? Because she was an actress, improvising her way through the days?

"Do you need a place to stay?"

"Do you have a place?" But Billy had asked only in conversation, not with any desire to offer a pillow and a blanket. Oh, no, he possessed no urge to help Mrs. Regina Glume, unless of course they came across the bracelet: He'd give her a hand with the clasp.

"You do have a place to stay, don't you, Regina?"

She stopped and quickly her face changed, falling a bit, softening into a little girl's; there was a quiver in her lip and a sigh that seemed to sink her chest. She looked around, ahead and behind, wide eyes darting at every rustle in the night; a bird was in a wisteria bush and the shaking leaves caused her to start. "I went back to him tonight," she began.

"To Donny?"

She nodded, chin lowered, and she said something and Billy

had to say, "Sorry, what'd you say?" and she repeated herself: "At first it was real nice, at first he was just so happy to see me home, and he opened up a big bottle of champagne, the kind with the orange label, French, and we were drinking and he put on his favorite Journey CD and he was holding me and we were dancing in the living room, something we only did on our first night together, and he opened a second bottle, and the night was better than it had ever been and he kissed my cheek and said, 'You're the most beautiful girl in Boston,' and I said, 'Ah, Donny, do you mean it, do you really mean it this time?' And he said he did and he squeezed me harder than he ever squeezed me, harder than he'd ever squeezed another girl, or so he said, and we were just so close it was like we were one and just then he pushed me away and shouted, 'What's that smell?' 'What smell, Donny? What're you talking about?' 'I smell another man on you!' That's what he yelled, and I told him he was crazy, told him he was smelling himself, and he told me I wasn't going to call him crazy, no bitch was going to call him crazy, and he knows what a man smells like and a man smells like you! That's what he said, and I just stood there scared, and it was only when he started shoving me around that I knew I better get out of there and I had just enough time to grab my purse before he flung the champagne bottles at me and it exploded against the wall and it was the loudest thing I ever heard, that green glass breaking up right by my ear, and it could've killed me, and I yelled that, 'You could've killed me!' And Donny looked at me with his eyes smaller than I'd ever seen and said, 'That's what I meant to do,' and so I ran out and flagged a taxi and got away from him and you know what the worst part of all this is?"

"What's that?" asked Billy.

"Donny was right." Now Regina was crying softly, a wadded tissue at her nose.

"Are you crazy, Regina? He wasn't right to try to kill you. No one has the right to do that." Billy took her hands.

"That's not what I mean." And then, "I *had* been with another guy. I couldn't help it. I didn't think I'd be seeing Donny tonight."

The windows in the town houses were black, and the shadows of the ginkgo trees swayed strangely on the sidewalk like a gray net thrashing with fish. Billy couldn't think of what to say next. He was more tired than he realized. It was as if the rum and Cokes and the Manhattan—who, *who* was it that bought him that Manhattan?—were returning to his head, as if a hand had reached out to dim the light on his miner's hat. At once the white cat from the rhododendron appeared, daintily crossing their path and then up a stoop.

"Where are you coming from?"

"I didn't know what else to do so I told the cab driver to take me to the Ritz."

"The Ritz?"

"Thought I'd hang in the bar for a while, let the time pass."

"I see. Anybody buy you a drink?"

"Not a soul."

"No one?"

"I asked one guy for a cosmopolitan, but he just looked at me and said, 'Sorry, Ma'am, I'm married.'"

This Billy understood. Her days had passed, and he came into an awareness about one thing in life: It happens in a flash, one day every guy in the bar wants to buy you a drink and the next day you've gone invisible. "Where were you headed just now?"

"I don't know."

"But why were you running earlier?"

She hesitated. Her eyes scanned Billy. "I didn't want to tell you."

"Tell me what?"

"He's out here looking for me."

"What are you talking about?"

"When I came out of the hotel I saw him pulling up in his Camaro, back to where it all started. I started running. I don't know but I don't think he saw me. Oh god, I hope the bartender didn't tell him anything. Do you think the bartender would've told him I was there?"

Never had Billy seen anything like it: the fear incandescent in her eyes, the tremor in her skin, the way she stood on the balls of her feet as if ready to flee. Her damp hands gripped him, and he could feel her moisture seep through his shirt; he tried to shake her away, pushing harder than he meant because she lost her balance but then righted herself; and in this instant of dislocation, in the cone of light cast from a street lamp, the bruises presented themselves to Billy brighter than before: the fingerprints stained into the flesh of her throat, the uriney yellow in her upper arm surrounding the faint dent of a vaccination scar, the pinkie that hung at a funny angle, crushed and almost dead. And if she had smelled of a man earlier in the evening, now she emitted the musk of panic.

She hugged Billy, in an annoying way that reminded him of his mother: There'd been a day not long ago when he declared that he'd no longer accept affection from her, although he wasn't sure why he'd said it. *Please don't touch me. Not in public,* he'd said, or Nina had said, or his mother had said to him and Nina; who had said it first? He couldn't be sure anymore.

They were on a street corner two blocks from home. The night was becoming chillier; a breeze knocked a potato chip bag across their feet. Now Billy wished he'd accepted one of the offers for a ride home. *I'm parked around back,* the pilot had said, pinching his mustache. *We can catch a taxi,* the doctor had said, lifting the cuff of his sweater to check the time. But Billy wasn't ready to leave the bar with a man, not yet. To tell the truth, Billy hadn't even kissed a man, but he pretended otherwise. No, I shouldn't, he had said. The pilot had kissed Billy's hand goodbye. The doctor had rubbed the bone in Billy's neck. And, Roger, gray-skinned Roger: He was waiting outside Club Café, around the corner in his Japanese hatchback with the upholstery splitting apart, the passenger door open, waiting like a dirty old man. When he saw Billy, whose heart rapped away, Roger had asked in his singsongy voice, "Need a ride?" causing Billy to let out a small cry.

"Are you hungry? You look a little hungry," Regina said. "I'll buy you a coconut cruller if you like. Come with me to the doughnut shop. You and me, we'll wait for dawn together. There'll be a policeman in there and we'll be safe."

"Safe?"

"From Donny."

Billy felt as if he'd been yelling for a long time and now had lost his voice. "I already ate," he muttered.

"Do you know where we are?" Regina asked, her neck turning. "I'm kinda all turned around. Do you know this part of town?"

Billy looked to the sky. The fog had veiled the moon. He was cold, the thin cotton of his Easter shirt riffling in the breeze. "Um, sort of."

They had reached the corner of his block. He could see the weak light above his front door. Something in him, something distant and dull, ached. He lowered his eyes, a sense of late defeat entering him, and it was then that he saw the charm bracelet on the cement. "There it is!"

"What?"

She fell to her knees, and said she couldn't believe it, she never thought she'd actually find it, and here it was, and "Oh, Billy, help me put it on."

He knelt beside her, their knees touching, and the bracelet, heavier than it looked, felt cool. The clasp took, and it was there on the sidewalk that she cupped his face and kissed Billy, thanking him over and over, I can never thank you enough, her lips pecking at him, his forehead and his cheek, the tip of his nose, his mouth, his mouth again, and just at this moment a carburetor groaned in the night, and a car, low on the street, barreled down the block.

"Billy! It's Donny!"

But Billy didn't believe it. What was the likelihood?

"It's him, it's him!" And Regina was clawing at Billy, hugging him as if he were her shield, and Billy still couldn't make out whether the car was a Camaro or something else, and as he knelt on the sidewalk he permitted Regina to decide what to do next, and before he knew it he and she were tumbling into a lilac bush, peering through the leaves.

"Can he see us?"

Billy didn't know; the Camaro moved more slowly down the street than he had first perceived. Billy, uncomfortable, shifted his position, and the leaves shook viciously. Regina hissed at him to be still. Together they watched the Camaro approach the corner, and as it rolled to a stop, a long horrible groan emerged in the night: "Regina!"

Billy held his breath. He could dash out of the bush now and be on his way, leaving her there, and really it was the most sensible thing to do. What did he care? What did Donny Vickerman have against Billy? Nothing, he had nothing to do with this whole mess, and Billy now felt as though his adventure for the evening had come to a close and he was ready to call it a night. He turned his head toward her and saw the tears falling silently. She wiped her nose, the bracelet tinkling offensively.

"I'm going to go," he whispered.

"No, please! Wait with me!" It was a plea unlike anything he had heard, the icy desperation. It revolted him; such exigency he refused to believe would ever enter his own life: Once again he envisioned himself in a house in the California foothills, painting in his studio, the man he loved—more important, the man who loved Billy—on the terrace waiting for him. That was his future, and this night, this lilac bush was Regina's; and so it was time to say good-bye.

Then the Camaro was gone, down the street and around the corner, hunting for Regina elsewhere. Donny Vickerman hadn't seen them. Everything in the night was as it was before all this had started. The bed in the brownstone with the A-B-C sheets awaited Billy.

They crawled out of the lilac bush, only two doors from Billy's home. "Good night, Regina."

"Where are you going?"

"I'm leaving you."

"What do you mean? Where are you going? Why would you leave me? You don't have any place to go, either. Let's wait out the night together. Come on, Billy. How about that doughnut? It's on me."

"No, that's it for tonight. You go that way," he pointed in the direction of the park, "and I'll go this way."

"But why? Why do you want to leave me?" Her cheek landed in the crook of his neck, the tears hot, and a flinch moved through him: her dirty crying on his skin, which he cleaned so attentively with a sea sponge and honey-and-oats soap, staining his collar, he feared. She heaved, her breasts pressed against him, the hard nipples rubbing his own through the Easter shirt; her heat rose through the angora tank top and reached his nostrils, the pickled alcoholic smell, the salty odor of someone who'd been with a man, or two; Billy recognized that, recognized the scent that could have been his own. "I'm scared, Billy."

"There's nothing to be scared of."

"You don't know Donny."

"He's gone."

"He's just around the corner. He could return any minute. He'll kill me if he sees me."

"He won't kill you," and Billy found himself patting her wiry mass of hair, which on closer inspection resembled his not at all. Her nose was wet, and she sucked in the mucus; a bubble caught in her lips and popped against Billy's flesh.

He'd had enough. "You'll be fine."

More gasps, more moans, a crying stranger sprawled across his firm shoulder.

"Please let go of me," Billy said calmly.

"But he'll kill me!"

Billy *tisk*ed, in a way that his mother might while reading about a cancer foundation in *Town & Country*. Were it another night, another hour, later in Billy's life, he would have stopped thinking about himself and stroked the cheek of the woman. He would've said, You're right. Or, Come in and I'll make you a cup of coffee. But tonight was the wrong night for a transfer of sympathy from Billy. "You'll have to let go of me," he said.

"Don't leave me like this." Her fingers clasped his nape, her lips were on his throat, no longer resting but moving, pecking, hunting for his ear; her tongue followed, wet and shockingly cold, her groin thrusting at his, and she cried, "You're killing me, Billy, leaving me all alone out here." And then, "Please take me wherever you're going. Just take me with you tonight."

Gently, feigning respect, he tried to unwrap himself from her arms, but she was going on, her breath in his ear, about not wanting to die, not wanting to give old Donny the pleasure in watching her die. "You think I'm not serious, don't you, you don't think Donny's serious, do you, but I'll tell you, I've seen him do it, I've seen him pound someone two inches from death, and he's told me he'd do it to me one day, his fist so close to my nose I could smell the grime beneath his nails, and Billy, you have no idea, do you? You don't know what you're doing by leaving me out here. It's not long until dawn, wait with me. Or at least walk me to the doughnut shop, at least do that for me, Billy! *Billy!*"

Billy tried to listen but her words were blurry, rising into a shriek, and with the gasping sobs in his ear he'd need a Q-Tip to remove the spit, and why was he talking to her, who was this woman, why did Billy bother to waste another minute with her? She meant nothing to him. He couldn't help her, could he? And she couldn't help him, and shouldn't they part ways now, call it a night and all the rest . . . and what was she saying now? She'd never wish such a horror on Billy, and this night would come back to haunt Billy because one of these days he'd find himself in the same situation and there'd be nobody to help him. "You think everyone's going to treat you nice: Well, you're wrong, Billy. You're going to find yourself in a suite at the Ritz all pampered and paid for and with a knife against your throat, and then you'll know what I'm talking about. Then who's going to help you out, Billy? Who's going to answer your screams? No one, Billy, you're the type who'll die screaming all alone, and you'll think of me on that night, you'll be thinking of me and of fucking Donny's Camaro hunting *you!*"

Then quite unexpectedly Billy found himself at the foot of the stairs to his mother's house. He stopped and forcefully pulled himself away from Regina. He brushed the wrinkles out of his shirt and buried his hands in his pockets. The crumpled phone numbers felt like laundered lint, and Billy said, "I have to say good night now. This is home."

Regina froze. "What do you mean?"

"I live here."

"I don't understand."

"This is my home."

"How can you live here? I thought you said you were on the street."

"I live here with my mom and my sister." He knew how phony he must seem then, timidly mumbling a good-bye and offering his hand, trying to close the conversation politely, the only way he knew how—a handshake and a coy little smile had always worked for him, had done the trick even tonight at Club Café. And there between them hung Billy's fine-boned hand, silvery in the night, hovering, seemingly detached, like a lost hummingbird. They both looked at it, as if trying to decide who would take it, and finally Regina snatched it in her fist and shook it hard.

"Then just invite me in for a second, Billy. Until we're sure Donny's gone. Then I'll leave. I won't cause any trouble, Billy, but please let me in for a while. Billy, he's going to kill me."

"But everyone's asleep."

"Just until dawn. I'll leave before they wake up. They'll never know I was there. Billy, you don't understand, do you? He said he was going to kill me." She continued to shake his hand, the way Billy's father used to pump Billy's fist, up and down, forgetting to let go.

"Another time?" Billy offered. And then, "Maybe I could bring you a glass of water?"

"But I don't need any water. I need to hide from him. Billy, why are you doing this? Billy, have you ever been in trouble? Have you ever needed someone's help? I'm asking you for your help." Her face was streaked, but the trembling in her lip had stopped; something firm gave her face a new horrible shape.

"It's just that Mom and Nina are sleeping."

"Billy! I don't understand." Her cheeks burned, sweat shining in the down above her lip, nostrils raw, her nipples still hard through her sweater, the crotch of her skirt askew; an awful sight for Billy, awful for him to think that somehow he had caused this. No, he told himself it wasn't his fault. No one would ever confuse him with Donny.

"It's late; you'd wake my mom. She's a light sleeper. I was supposed to be home an hour ago." He checked his watch. "Two hours ago." He began to back his way up the stoop, one step and then another, groping the black iron rail, but Regina wouldn't release his hand. "Please let me go. If it's money you need—"

A furious cloud moved in and settled on her face. "This isn't a game! He has a gun, Billy. Donny keeps a couple of rifles in a case in the living room. Oh, god, Billy, he's driving around, he's going to come back up the street and find me. Billy, look what he's already done to me. Billy!" She was following him up the steps and showing him the bruises, holding up her arm, turning her neck like a dog submitting. "Why won't you let me in? Why don't you want to help save me?"

"I, I don't think I can." He heard the frightened voice of a little boy.

"Oh, god, Billy, please let me in!" She was yelling, the tendons leaping out on her throat, her ears as red as the maraschino cherries in all those cocktails at Club Café. They heard a car down the street, saw the sweep of its headlamps. The car moved slowly, a heaviness in its engine.

"It's him, Billy! It's Donny! Quick, let me in Billy. Let me in!"

Billy turned and ran to the top of the steps, reaching in his pocket for his house key. It was in there, beneath the phone numbers and the photo, a shopping mall photo, Roger had made Billy accept. "Remember me," Roger had said from the peeling bucket seat of his Japanese hatchback, the door open.

"Of course," Billy had giggled, not meaning it, intending to throw away the photo with its autumn-pond background in one of the wire trash bins in the park, where he should have turned around and taken another route the moment he heard the crackling noise in the rhododendron. And now here he was, at the top of his stoop, fighting off this woman, with her egg-shaped eyes overflowing with tears, with her tight lipless mouth, her tongue huge and bumpy with gray buds. "You're getting way too excited about this," he was yelling. "You're taking this way too far. I'm sorry about lying to you, but don't you see I can't help you?" And then, even more desperately, "Leave me alone."

The car continued to creep its way up the block. Why was it driving so slowly?

Billy found the key. But what if she pushed her way through the door, what if they both came tumbling into his mother's anteroom with the blue porcelain umbrella stand and the horse-hair foot mat? Regina would be in their house and . . . and, oh god, what was he going to do?

"Why don't you want to help me, Billy?" And then, with a mournful sob that Billy had heard only once before—the hour after his father left his mother slumped against the front door—"It isn't fair."

"I don't know, I don't know, but please. It's just that"—what did Billy want to say?—"I want to go up to my room and go to sleep. I want to forget all about this. Can't we do that? Can't we forget all about this?"

They were standing on the top stair now, eight steps above the sidewalk. Billy saw the orange parking tickets tucked beneath windshield wipers across the street, and saw the opposite row of brownstones, their polished brass knockers as bright as gold. A bird chirped and shook the leaves of a neighbor's holly bush. The car continued its creep in their direction. "I'm going to buzz my mother and have her call the police," he said, his voice turning calm and flat.

"Good, call the police. Do anything you want, just don't leave me out here. Billy, here he comes. It's Donny! Look, it's Donny, Billy, hurry, let's get inside!" And again, "Hurry!"

He raised his finger to the buzzer, moving it to the pearly white button with the pink light glowing behind, his fingertip turning up as Regina cried, "Don't leave me!" Her hand clamped down on the ball of his wrist, and now Billy's free hand was trying to ply her away, shaking her arm until they found themselves in a tug-of-war, yanking on one another, pulling on each other's arms. They were teetering on the top of the stoop, but Billy wasn't going to let this happen! Not Billy Henderson, who tonight had swatted away like flies all those men at Club Café, not Billy who could handle a doctor, a pilot, a logging company executive, *and* a freak with no eyebrows whacking his thing beneath the steering wheel of his Japanese hatchback.

Billy's back was pressed to the door. Only the woman's toes were on the top step, the weight of her body leaning into the air above the stairs, suspended by the pull of Billy's attempts to free himself. The car continued its slow rumble up the street. Regina was trying to drag Billy off the step, away from the door, where inside his sister and his mother were sleeping beneath their eiderdowns, their hair fanned around their pillow-creased faces. If only his mother would wake up and lift her Roman shade and look out at the scene occurring this very instant on her stoop. Again the woman yanked, and Billy yanked back. "Why are you doing this to me?" he cried.

"You're not going to get away with this. I don't care what happens anymore, you're just not going to get away with this," she was screaming, her face blotchy. "You might as well be dead and the world would be all the same, you know that, don't you?"

"What are you talking about?"

"It makes you think, doesn't it?" And then, with glassy rage: *"Doesn't it!"*

Something inside Billy split in two, and the next thing he knew a little electronic *click!* came from the intercom box and his mother's voice was saying, "Who's there? What's going on?"

Billy snapped his wrist free of the woman's hands, his left hand flying back, the round face of the watch breaking against a brick, and with the sound of the glass smashing it seemed to Billy that time came to a stop, and all the world was his to see.

Regina swooped her arms in circles, trying to regain her balance before soaring in a neat arc to the bottom step. Her arms flapped slowly like a huge ugly bird's. Her oily eyes met Billy's, and his mother's tense voice asked, "Billy, is that you?"

Billy no longer knew if it was he; he couldn't believe it was he who was witnessing Regina fall to her death, *sending* her to her death on the sidewalk cracked by the roots of the ginkgo tree, cracked as her head certainly would be in the next second of Billy's life. At once the car pressed closer, its headlights lasers in the fog. In a flash Billy could think of only how this would end his life as he knew it, of his jail time for killing Regina, his future years at the old Victorian prison out on Route 2 where his bony ass would stand out like a bull's-eye. Billy was killing someone, and you know what, he might as well be killing himself. He felt something in him shift: a hazy swirl in his head like the rush of the Manhattan, a devouring touch running down his spine. He heard his mother's voice, raw with sleep, "What's happening to you, Billy?" He looked into Regina's face, into her dull eyes already lifeless and still, and as she closed her lids—resigned to the fact that this indeed was happening to her, that indeed Billy was shoving her into a terrible plunge—just then the woman's flailing hand, the left one with the bracelet with the stars and the single fat moon, caught hold of the railing and snagged her already tumbling body, halting her fall. The car passed them, a silver Buick driven by a white-haired lady in a white-fur hat peering over the wheel. And with that, Billy Henderson, not a week past his eighteenth birthday, pushed himself through the front door and turned the bolt behind him. Out of the sodden night, he landed a foot on the step and his hand on the polished rail, the broken watch shifting, and mounted the stairs to his bed.

LIVING TOGETHER

Alex Tuck wondered if he should return the cat, thinking he could no longer fit her into his life, and now here she was, Joan, the size of a small beagle and with a leathery ear ripped from an alley fight, coughing up a slimy ball of fur. He turned to Guy, whose lip was curling just then, his nose, a little boy's nose on the face of a man, twitching. See, this was why Alex shouldn't have taken Joan from his sister. He couldn't manage. He couldn't manage her.

Guy set down the last box. His knees cracked and the brittle sound of it made Alex think of how much older Guy was: more than fifteen years, Guy closer to forty than not, and hair dusted with gray, and bones that spoke, and a look in his handsome dimpled face of—how else could Alex describe it?—a powerful man who could break any heart he chose to fondle and squeeze.

"Does she always do that? Puke up like that?"

"No, not always." Alex's hands were up in the air, protesting something.

"Don't you think you should've told me about it before you moved in?" Guy's face was still, his eyes rocks of gold, and Alex felt a jolt through him—had he already messed things up with his new roommate?—but then Guy was laughing, winking, scratching Joan's black tail with one hand and his own head with the other. He touched the cat's whiskers and then the white patch on her belly. "Hey, Alex, relax buddy." A smile cracked Guy's face: lips, and the steak of a tongue, dimly purple. "I had a roommate in college once who had a cat. She sort of looked like Joan, except her name was Betty, as in Ford. She loved to lick the wineglasses in the sink."

Alex scooped Joan into his arms. She was purring, and her fur was damp from the mist greasing the city outside, and Alex just then noticed the hair on Guy's knees, hair like fur, already sun-bleached from the season's first days at the beach—Provincetown, Guy had told Alex; a beach town on the fist of Cape Cod where men wore swimsuits the size of cocktail napkins, Guy had explained, or nothing at all, and where anyone, yes, anyone, could find love for the night. "You'll have to come along with me one weekend," Guy had said, when they first met, just one week ago.

"What happened to her?"

"Who?"

"Betty the cat?"

"Oh, Betty? Oh god, it was awful. Oh god, I haven't thought about it for a long time. One day when my roommate and I were at our marketing class, Betty must have been playing around because when we got home we found her with her collar caught on the knob of a kitchen drawer. Poor Betty, hanging there, her neck snapped. Dead like that," and Guy snapped his fingers, which were thick and backed by the same golden strands of fur.

Alex didn't know what to say. His eye wandered to the galley kitchen, where a lone frying pan hung on a rack. Would Joan do something like that here? She wasn't even his cat, really, but his older sister's. He'd taken on Joan only in the last year, after protesting about not having the time, about not being home enough, about not having room for her in his life. "Just do me this one favor," Nan had said, bandaged in her hospital room.

On a Boston street gripped by gentrification, at the top floor of a renovated brownstone, the apartment had plenty of room for the two men, one young, the other less so. Enough room for them and the cat, though they would have to share the bathroom, with its bin of skin-care products and its sink caked with white droppings of toothpaste. But the yellow pine floors and pale gray walls and the high ceilings added to the sense of space—certainly the two men would not stumble over each other here. Bay windows in the living room framed a view—if you stretched your neck—of the slim John Hancock tower, which just now was shimmering with sunlight needling through the mist. And then through the skylight more sun appeared, falling

on Alex and Guy; the spitty rain was lifting, the green-and-blue
burst of early summer returning, and there he was, Alex, just
out of college, still, at twenty-two, filling in the gaps of his frame,
all bone and angst, as he thought of it; and there was Guy, a
man no taller than Alex but somehow more present, arms
stretching the sleeves of his T-shirt, which read P-TOWN VOLLEY-
BALL over the breast, and one big toe, bony and tan, scratching
the other, and the mesh of gym shorts catching, and displaying,
the bulk and shift of Guy's thigh. Yes, there they were, Alex boiling up under his sweater buttoned to the throat and in the sun,
which now flooded the skylight and shined down on them, the
two of them, in that awkward moment when two people, two
strangers, realize that indeed they will be living together.

It was only the second time they had met. Alex had lived
through this moment once before with his freshman roommate—a scene of common hope showing up in their mutually
tentative grins, in the way the two boys turned away from each
other as they undressed that first night. Hope that this other
person would remain reasonable. Hope that the stranger,
whose bed sat four or five feet from Alex's, would not crack and
lose it in the night, slouching in the direction of cruelty. Alex
supposed married couples, his own parents for that matter,
must also share this moment: After the honeymoon, after the
romance, his mother must have looked at his bearded father at
least once and thought, "Don't turn on me." Alex would've
asked, but his father was dead, long dead.

A water stain, scaly and yellow, spread on the wall from the
skylight to the floor. Rain must have seeped in during a winter
past. At one spot the paint had blistered into a circle the size of a

hand, and Alex was surprised to see it, puzzled that he hadn't noticed the damage when he'd first visited the apartment. He had also missed the urine stain on the carpet, and the flash of gold in Guy's molars.

"So, here we are," said Alex, and he laughed, though Guy could have mistaken it for a gasp. It struck Alex that this was happening to him now, at last, that he was actually in the middle of this: a new apartment with a new roommate in a new city, and tomorrow he would start his first job; he thought of the empty desk waiting, with its silent phone, with the Rolodex hanging limply with blank cards. It was a new life for a young man in search of a new life; it occurred to him just then that no one knew him or who he was or where he came from and no one had met his sister, thin in a nightgown, or his mother, with her hair swooped up like a meringue. He knew he would spend the next several months of his life introducing himself, and he knew—although he couldn't explain it, were you to ask—that it would never again be like this, never again would life feel like this, with so much sprawled ahead, life ajar. So this is how I'll be living, he thought, looking around, and there was Guy again, sitting on the steps that led to the roof deck, pulling on his gym socks, his legs agape.

Alex could feel the sweat on his forehead; he told himself he was too excited, and he wiped at the dew above his lip. He patted his brow with the handkerchief he had spent last night ironing, this one and his dozen others and his T-shirts, all white and blank, discarded at the first sign of yellow stain beneath the arm, and his gym shorts, which he had bought recently because a boy in college, not quite a friend, a boy with a wardrobe of sheer blousy shirts and an older boyfriend in New York, had said, "You'll have to join a gym when you get to Boston. You were planning on joining a gym, weren't you, Alex?" But his own sweat bothered Alex, the clinginess, the lingering scent, the way it pasted his clothes to his skin and revealed the angles, the pink, of his somehow childlike body. "A gym?" Alex had said. "Yes, I've already signed up," he had lied. But what would Alex do at a gym?

Yet Alex knew that soon, none too soon, he would find out. Was Guy on his way to the gym just now?

"You look hot," said Guy, tying his sneakers and then standing and laying a hand on Alex's shoulder. "How about something to drink?" And then, "Hey, do you want to go to the gym with me? Go for a workout and then a steam?"

They had met through a service called Rainbow Roommates recommended by the boy in college, Patrick, whose hair was dyed a raspberry red. "You fill out a form of what you're looking for in a roommate. You know, your likes, your dislikes. If you're a smoker or not. Be sure to put down how anal you are," Patrick had said, giggling in that girlish way of his. To Alex the whole thing sounded like blind dating, something he had never done, but it excited him—the idea of calling someone, and then meeting him in his apartment, an actual stranger, just anybody who could afford the sixty-dollar fee. And then with limited information—the neatness of the part through his hair, the firmness of his handshake, the order of the pillows on the living room sofa, the potential stability that his job as a computer salesman implied, all of this plus any display of kindness, or cruelty, for that matter—a decision had to be made whether or not Alex could live with this man. It made no sense, really, that people could proceed this way, the risks were too high—*he could be an utter slob . . . he could go through my things and read my diary . . . he could ask me to join him in his sleigh bed late one night*—but what else could Alex do? Where else would Alex live? Back in California? Back in his mother's house? Back down the tiptoey hall that connected Alex's bedroom to his sister's? Alex needed to get on with his new life, he needed an apartment and a roommate, a place he could afford on his first-time salary, a roommate who would not only hand him a key but also make room for his cat, Saint Joan, as he sometimes called her, and Boston was about as far as he could hope from Pasadena, where his mother still lived, where his sister had returned to, and he knew no one in this city, in this state, no one except an ex of Patrick's, whom Patrick had urged Alex to look up—*you'll like Timmy, he reminds me of you*—which didn't turn out to be the case; Alex knew no one at all until now, no one but Guy, who was throwing his leather-and-mesh lifting gloves into his backpack and saying, "Let's go to the gym. Joan'll be all right. Leave her and let's head out for a workout." And then, "Come on, Alex, everyone knows that the first thing you do after finding a place to live is sign up for the gym." And then, finally, with a second hand on Alex's other shoulder, "Hey, Alex. Is everything all right? Are you going to be all right?"

———

But Alex turned down the trip to the gym, and in his new room he tried to unpack. He hung what he could in the closet, but it was shallow, a single short pipe and two hooks, and he'd have to store most of his clothes in boxes beneath the bed. "I've got some extra room in my closet," Guy offered, standing in the door frame, his backpack hanging from a fist. Alex declined, saying he didn't really need any extra space. "Most of this stuff I don't wear anymore." This wasn't true, but might as well be, he realized, because he knew that part of piecing together this new life would come from buying a new set of clothes—a tank top for the summer, a pair of cargo-pocketed shorts—that would make him look more like one of *them*.

Then Joan padded between Guy's legs into the bedroom. "How long have you had her?" She sat in the space between Alex and Guy, looking from one to the other and back.

"Just under a year." Alex was rolling his winter socks and folding his cardigans into a pile. These he would store beneath the bed, in a box labeled BOOKS where he would also hide his diary and his thumbed stash of daddy-son fantasy magazines.

"Where'd she come from?"

"She used to be my sister's."

"Why'd she give her up?"

Alex's room overlooked an alley, and through the window came the yelling of a man and a woman, a couple shrieking over a jealousy: "Would you stop looking at my sister like that!"

"She almost died and couldn't take care of her anymore."

Alex continued with the pile of sweaters. When Guy was gone he would begin folding his boxer shorts; he couldn't bring himself to fold his underwear in front of his roommate, not just yet. A second shriek came from the alley, this time a single heaving sob. And then, just barely, "I can't believe you did that." Almost a year had passed since Nan had tried to kill herself, and the note she left had asked him to take care of Joan. But Nan survived, and it never occurred to Alex that Saint Joan would become his, except that was what his mother decided would be best. "She should live with you," his mother had said, and at first Alex didn't know who she was referring to: Who was the she? "She seems to really like you." And then, "It's like she's in love with you, that cat is."

It was a year before that—a little more than two years ago—when Nan had first adopted Joan. She was living in Santa Monica at the time, writing copy for an advertising agency two blocks from the beach. Alex's mother liked to tell her friends that her daughter was practically famous: She had written those TV commercials for Pig Pig Bacon, the ones with the lovers nibbling opposite ends of a strip of ham, the one with the jingle that almost everyone in the country—or so it seemed to his mother, to Nan, even to Alex himself—was singing just then.

After Nan adopted the cat, Alex went home to visit his family. One night he decided to sleep on Nan's sofa rather than at his mother's, and there they were in Nan's apartment, Alex and Nan, separated by five years, the older sister a prettier version of her brother yet the two nearly identical in size: she the strong impressive woman, he the slight rail of a man; that night, that one night, during Alex's spring break, in the downpour of a California March storm, the gutters overflowing above Nan's window, there in her living room, with the shelf of video boxes, each a clip of one of her commercials, there they spoke, the two siblings, about this and that, about the rain, about their mother, about the new cat. "She's the size of a small dog," Alex had exclaimed when he first tried to load her into his arms. "She thinks she's a puppy," Nan had said, her fingers, tan from a recent visit to the sun bed, raking Joan's fur, picking at a knot in her tail.

"I would have thought you would've wanted a Persian or some fancy cat like that." And Nan—whose beauty no one in the world would argue with, not a soul in the world—had replied, "What would make you say that?"

Yes, what would make Alex say that? "What's that thing on her paw?"

"Oh, that?" His sister inspected the bald patch on the cat's front paw. "She has this weird habit of chewing her own foot. Another indication that she thinks she's a dog."

Sometimes when he closed his eyes, he couldn't remember what his sister looked like: She was a figure, alive and huge, with a blank oval of a face; someone had scratched it out. What made her beautiful? Sometimes he would ask himself, but he could never answer the question; he'd have to pull out an old photo—the two of them on a picnic in Lacy Park or hiking beneath the summit of Mount Wilson, alone, away from the world—to remind himself that her eyes were green, the green of late summer when the underside of a leaf, overturned in the wind, reveals itself as blue.

For many months Nan had been inviting Alex to visit her in her new apartment in Santa Monica. "Whenever you come out, why not spend a night or two with me? Why spend all that time with Mom? She drives you crazy."

"She drives you crazy, too."

That night—that only night Alex slept on his sister's couch—they stayed up late. Joan (was this the first time he ever thought of her as Saint Joan?) moved from Nan's lap to Alex's and back. Nan proceeded with a conversation in which he added very little, or that was how it felt to Alex. How old was he that night? Oh, only twenty, just twenty, and yet at certain instances he felt like a child, as if he had no more experience with the grime of

the world than an eight-year-old; and at other times, other
nights, tonight perhaps, he felt old, a soul wise and sound and
still. And perhaps he felt both at once, perhaps just then in his
life Alex was beginning to perceive the doubleness, the inexhaustible doubleness, of his life. This and that, all at the same
time; and here they were, Alex, twenty and still only shaving
once a week, and Nan, with a curtain of blond hair falling around
her face, in a sleeveless red sweater that shaped her breasts like
the skin over the meat of an apple. Was she wearing anything
beneath the sweater? He didn't think so, and then she cracked a
window—*It's warm tonight*—and with the breeze faintly salty
from the ocean running across their skin, her skin, Alex became
certain that the answer was no. She was in a pair of khaki shorts,
with a little side pocket where she would store, were she on a
trek through a forest, an army knife and a small sack of raisins.
Why did Alex have that thought about his sister just then, about
what she might pack away in the side pocket of her shorts? He
had never trekked with her, never shared a tent with her, never
lain awake with her as the wind ran across their nylon sleeping
bags. So why imagine her in shorts and hiking boots, with
raisins stored away? Had he dreamed of this? Had this, all of
this, flitted through his dreamer's mind?

They sat opposite each other on the two white sofas their
mother had bought for Nan from a catalog. Alex curled his legs
beneath him, and if he'd had a tail it would be tucked up too.
Nan lay spread out on her back, her orange toenails dangling
over the sofa and her arm flinging about as if it were searching
for a box of chocolates on the coffee table. "So, I've been dating
this guy," she began.

"That's great." Alex pulled his knees to his chest. "Who is he?"

"His name is Carter. He's a writer, a screenwriter. He just sold his first script."

"That sounds great."

"He is," and Nan turned her head to her brother and smiled, and then shook herself almost imperceptibly, as if a shiver were creeping up her spine.

"How long have you been seeing him?"

"About four months."

"Does Mom like him?"

"Mom? Oh, he hasn't met Mom."

Sometimes he couldn't imagine talking to Nan if she weren't his sister. He felt that way about his mother, less often, but even so. They weren't people he naturally would want to get to know. At Christmas dinner a few years ago, when he was a little drunk on grog, he blurted out at the table that the only thing he had in common with them was food.

"Where'd you meet him?" Alex said.

"Who?"

"Carter?"

"Oh, Carter. Where'd I meet Carter? It's the funniest story. It's one of those times when you can't believe how small the world is, when you think you must be related to the whole world because it's just so small. But I'll tell you later. It's a long story. Such a *long* story."

And then Nan said, with one hand buried in the fur of the cat, "By the way, Alex, are you gay?"

"Yes."

"Yeah, I thought so. I was just wondering." She curled a strand of hair behind her ear. "It doesn't bother me one bit."

"It doesn't bother me, either."

"But I wouldn't tell Mom. I'm not sure how she would take it."

"She already knows."

He stood, moving to the window. Her apartment overlooked an alley, and in the carport below Alex could see Nan's little red convertible and the garbage bins chained to a post. He didn't want to talk to his sister anymore, not about this. He was hot, and he opened the window further, and a veil of damp salt air fell across his face and he wondered why she would talk to him like this. He didn't like to move into the realm of intimacies with Nan. To tell the truth, he didn't trust her. When they were young, when Nan was twelve, she used to invite Alex to play dress-up with her whenever their mother was out on an errand. Together they'd put on old flowered gowns that their mother could no longer fit into. Alex would fix Nan's hair with yellow ribbons, and next Nan would clip into Alex's hair white barrettes painted with green butterflies. They would dance to the radio, and Nan always said it was all right, it's okay for you to play like a girl, Alex, it doesn't matter. And Alex loved the fun of pretending, he loved the crush of chiffon beneath him as he sat down to a make-believe dinner party. Then one night, as Alex and Nan stood in the kitchen with their mother, Nan proudly said, "Alex likes to dress up with me. He likes to put on your dresses, Mom. Especially that old orange velvet one, the one you spilled chocolate pudding on." Alex's mother quietly set down her pocketbook and took his wrists, one in each hand. "You're not your sister," she said, shaking. "Why are you acting like your sister?"

———

That first night in the apartment, Alex and Guy ordered Chinese food. They carried the little white cardboard boxes to the roof, where there was a rotting deck and patio chairs chained to the chimney and pitted with rust. It was a few minutes past sunset, the sky bright at the rim, a half moon arranging itself for the evening. Just beyond was the Prudential tower, erect and poked with antennae, and over there the financial district, the offices twinkling with people uncertain if they should call it a night. On a deck down the block three women were tending a flaring barbecue. Beyond them a man and a woman, erased to silhouette, pressed together in embrace.

Guy was talking about his past boyfriends. "Lewis was a copy-machine repairman. He came into my office a few times with smudges of toner on his nose and then we exchanged numbers. When we started dating I found out he wasn't really a copy-machine repairman but actually a poet. So I convinced him he had too much talent to be wasting his time fixing copiers. His poems were amazing; I can't describe them, but they were amazing. He started writing a collection of poetry with a poem about every tiny part of my body. You know, a poem on the skin at the cheekbone, one on the hair at the wrist bone, a poem about my second toe."

Guy stopped, as if to give Alex a chance to comment, but Alex liked the story too much to interrupt. "Anyways," Guy went on, "he quit his job and lived with me for nearly two years, writing poetry while I was at work. He used what's now your room as his study, setting up a little desk and everything. He said he was working on an epic. In fact, he said he was rewriting *The Faerie Queene*. I paid for everything, and he wrote during the day and did most of the housework, which was handy because I'm not so good with that sort of stuff. But I can't believe I put up with him, supporting him like that. I mean, without realizing it, all of a sudden I was keeping a man, which is definitely not the type of guy I am. But you know what? Sometimes I really miss his cooking. I mean, every night I'd come home to something different: sashimi, tacos."

Alex considered the complexities of living together and the issues of money and chores and privacy and love. He could remember the days when he was very young and only his father's name appeared on the family's checking account. His mother sometimes could not take Alex to the grocery store because she had forgotten to ask his father to sign a check made out to El Rancho; she'd have to wait until the next day, unless she forgot again to ask his father to sign the two or three checks as he shuffled out of the house into the early-morning glare. His mother's face often tightened with nerves as she explained the checks: the grocery store, the shoe repair, tuition was due. Once Alex heard her say, "But it's my money, for god's sake." That was before he died; just before the car he and Nan were in swerved off the road.

"Finally, one day I came home from work," Guy continued. "And my so-called boyfriend said, 'Honey, I've got something to show you,' and he held up this little paperback book with a drawing on the cover of a boy in khaki shorts and no shirt and a yellow kerchief around his throat sitting on the knee of an older man, a scoutmaster, some guy with a chevron on his sleeve. The book was called *Boys Scout*. And I said, 'What's that?' and he said, 'It's mine, I wrote it. Go on, open it up,' and then it hit me, like a big old frying pan on the head, that all that time he'd spent at home, all that time I'd paid for—*for the sake of literature,* as he kept putting it—during all that time, he'd been writing a porn novel. And you know what, Alex? With his first check—which wasn't so big, mind you—he up and moved. You know what he said? He said I don't understand a writer's mind. And then he was gone, didn't even take his little desk. That desk in your room, that was his. And every once in a while when I'm in New York on business I make a little side trip into a triple-X shop and buy one of his new books. He writes three or four a month now, and has a lot of pen names like Raymond Kenneth Hedgspoon III and Jack Luck." Guy stopped to fish a sesame shrimp out of the cardboard carton. "And you know what the worst part of all of this is?"

"What?"

"Those novels are pretty good. I try my best not to get horny when I read them. I mean, I'm still angry at him and everything, but by the second page, even before I know it, I'm sitting there with my old coconut in my fist."

Alex mumbled something that Guy could have heard as, "It was called *Boys Scout*?" But what Alex really said, or should have said, were he an honest fellow, was: "I've read *Boys Scout*."

But Guy seemed to trust Alex's awkwardness. He showed no distaste for the nervousness, for the mumbled words, for the way Alex's eyes would fail to meet his own. Alex supposed that this was what had first convinced him that Guy would make a fine roommate. He didn't seem like the type of man who would mind Alex and his ways. When he first came to see the apartment, Alex had flushed red as a wound when Guy asked a few questions people should know about each other before they move in. "Do you sleep around a lot?" Guy had inquired. "I'm not making any judgment calls, but I suppose I should know about it in advance if you think you'll be bringing home a different guy every night."

"Oh, no. It's not like that. I mean. No, not every night, not . . . not . . . not—"

But he couldn't continue.

"Well, give me an idea of what to expect. On average, how many people do you sleep with a month?"

"I . . . I don't really know."

"What do you mean you don't really know?"

"I mean, I don't know what you mean. What you're asking me." And then Alex needed to sit on the sofa and he brought a pillow needlepointed with a lavender lambda to his chest.

"Are you all right?"

"No, I'm fine. Just tired is all."

And Guy went to the kitchen and returned with a glass of water. With the first sip Alex felt better, and Guy seemed to know to talk about something else.

Except for one last comment: "Of course, if you get a boyfriend, something long-term, that would be different. In that case, he'd be welcome to stay over. I wouldn't mind sharing the bathroom with someone if you're in love."

"Of course," Alex said. "Of course that would be different."

"And the same goes for me," Guy offered. "I won't be bringing home too many tricks. Just the ones where there's something indicating that first hint of love."

———

For nearly a year Alex had lived by himself in Tokyo in an apartment with blue paper parasols hanging from the ceiling and a mouse that came up through the pipes to nibble on the bathroom soap. He was there studying history at Keio University, his junior year abroad, away from the little world of college and his half-friend Patrick, away from home, away from everyone he knew. It was a year when his telephone rarely rang, and he could lose himself in the orange brick library until closing and there was no one to ask him where he'd been. It was a year when he could meet a man, and then another, men sometimes twice his age, late at night at Kinsmen, the upstairs bar in Ni-Chome, and return to his apartment with the stain of dawn and no one would ever know how his evening had passed. With whom it had passed. Alex was alone, and he knew that never again would the world permit him to live so alone. For the first time he wondered if it was what he wanted, this isolation, or if some sort of attachment to another would one day appeal to him. Then late one summer night, when the humidity clung to his skin, Alex was taking a cold bath. The phone rang, and Alex ran to answer: "*Moshi moshi.*"

"Nan's gone and tried to kill herself," his mother blurted out, as if she also wanted to say, "So what do you think of that?"

Alex immediately felt repulsed by his nudity. How could he talk to his mother without any clothes on? About Nan? He crouched on the tatami mat like a bird dropping an egg. At his feet lay a glossy, thumbed magazine that he'd planned to use later that night. With a quick snap Alex closed his thighs, tucking away his genitals.

"Alex, oh, it's awful," his mother cried. "She flung herself through the front window of a restaurant. She just stood back on the sidewalk, took a running start, and flew through the air and then through the glass, crashing in on the tables. It was late at night. Something must've made her lose control." His mother paused. "I guess she cracked."

He opened his mouth, as if he were about to scream, but nothing came out. Both at once it felt as if his heart were racing and coming to a halt. "What do you suppose made her do it?"

"I was hoping you might have some idea," she said, sniffling, and Alex imagined her nose against the shoulder of her robe.

"But something must have caused it."

"How am I supposed to know? She's all stitched up now and can't talk."

"How is she?"

"It looks like she's going to be all right." Again the doubleness of life: relief and regret flooding his chest simultaneously. Was it possible to love his sister in more than one way? he asked himself, he had often asked himself. To love her and hate her and love her yet again, all in the same compressed instant of his life. Where did it come from, the doubleness, the perpetual flip-flopping of emotion? Would it ever relent? What was it Patrick used to say? The man you love will build you up and ruin you all at the same time, so just get used to it, my sweet Alexandra.

Then Alex heard his mother *tisk*ing at Joan. She continued rattling into the phone and at Joan: *And who's going to take care of this sweet old cat?* Again Alex strained to picture his sister, to imagine her hurling herself through the window. Yet all he could see was the body of an athletic woman sprinting down the sidewalk, a naked muscled physique like that of an Olympic swimmer topped off with Alex's own shallow, over-heated face.

His mother wanted him to come home at once. "Won't you

come back to see her? It would cheer her up. She's buried in bandages, and she can't move yet and she can't speak because she has so many stitches in her lips. It would make her so happy to see you, I just know it. Right now, you're the only thing she has. You and me."

"Mom, I can't. My courses are really tough and I can't skip any lectures. I still have a lot of research to get done before I leave here. I'll be home in five weeks."

"But couldn't you come home for a week? Oh, Alex, please. For once won't you change your plans?"

"I can't."

And he didn't.

But every day his mother would call from the hospital room and give her account of what she thought Nan would like to say to him. "You know, I was thinking, Alex. When Nan gets married—the music can make or break a wedding—and I was thinking about what we should have at Nan's wedding."

"But is Nan even dating anyone?" Alex said, worried about the cost of the telephone call.

"A mother has to be prepared to take care of the details of her children's lives. Isn't that right, Nan? Your sister just nodded in agreement with me, Alex. Besides, Nan just recently began dating again one of her old boyfriends, a nice young man who wants to be a writer. A boy named Carter."

"How is she feeling today?"

"Carter is such a nice boy. And handsome, too. You know how they met? This was over a year ago, but do you know how they met?"

"But how is Nan today? Is she any better?"

"It's the funniest story. Don't you want to hear it?"

"But is she any better? Have the doctors said anything today?"

"Oh, she's the same but a little better I suppose. Less"—and this she whispered—"sedated."

"Did the doctors tell you anything?"

"Anyway, you'll never believe where they met."

Alex gave up. "Where'd they meet?"

"In your bedroom."

"In my bedroom?"

"Well, you know how I sometimes rent out the house to film crews and television producers and the like. Well, one day I got a call asking if they could film a commercial for a mortgage bank, and they needed a boy's bedroom—you know, something real boy-boy, with pennants on the wall and stuff. They asked if I had a son and if his room was available. I said I sure do and it sure is and so on the day of the shoot I had to be out of town so Nan agreed to watch over things and the young man who wrote the commercial's script is Carter, and that's why they met in your bedroom. Isn't that funny?"

"Not really."

"Oh, Nan thought it was. She knew that would wind you up."

"Well, it doesn't."

"Oh, Alex, why do you have to take everything so seriously?"

"What else have the doctors told you?"

"One last thing, Alex," his mother said. "Nan and I are stuck on something."

"What's that?"

"What's that organ march by Krebs, you know the one, the

one that goes *dum dum dum dum*. Oh, what's that called? Nan and I were talking—well, I was the one doing the talking—about her wedding, in the event she would ever marry Carter one day, and we were talking about music and what should be played at the ceremony and right at the same time we both thought of this piece by Krebs but we couldn't think of what it's called. Shoot, you know the one I'm talking about, *dum dum dum dum*. Her doctors think she'll be out of here by the time you get back from Japan. She has this terrific lady plastic surgeon. *Dum dum dum*, damn it, Alex, help me. It starts with a *W*."

But what was Nan thinking just then, lying there beneath the gauze, IV drip to her right, her eyes peering out? His sister, now faceless in a body bandage. He couldn't bring himself to tell his mother that the piece she was thinking of was called "Wachet auf." Instead, this somehow reminded him of the dinner table of his youth and the time his mother announced, "Nan is going to love having a playmate this summer." Without informing anyone, Mrs. Tuck had invited a girl with chapped shins from the South of France to live with them for June and July. When Nan, who was twelve at the time, found out, she sulked for a week, until the girl's plane landed, and then Nan started to scream. "I thought Nan would've loved you, Nathalie," Mrs. Tuck had to eventually say as she drove the bony child back to the airport after only eleven days in America. "I must have been wrong." But Alex never got the chance to say that *he* would have loved to have had the little girl stay and help him by sharing the daily alarm of living with Nan.

———

After dinner on the roof, Alex set out for a walk in his new neighborhood. He wanted to find the market, the florist, the coffee shop, the video store. On Columbus Avenue, in the yellow cone of a street lamp, he stopped to watch a young woman juggle sacks of groceries, her dry cleaning dangling from a pinkie and her mail between her teeth as she struggled with her keys. Cars were parked, some of them waving neon orange tickets beneath their wipers. Diners filled the window of the Japanese restaurant, conductorly chopsticks in the air. Men passed, men in nylon running pants with snaps at the ankles, men in tank tops stretched across their shaved chests, men peering out beneath baseball caps, beneath tidy haircuts, beneath eyebrows pruned and shaped by the tweezer. There were many men, most a few years older than Alex and some Alex's age, moving up the street, headed somewhere with their backpacks, with their thick-soled sneakers, with their shoulders meaty with muscle and tattooed. To the gym, Alex knew, and he followed them, although in truth there weren't that many, just four or five, but it felt to Alex, on that first night, as if there were more, as if he'd seen the world that would become his, and indeed it heaved and sighed with the fullness of a world: a street, a market, a neighbor with her groceries, a parking ticket, a pack of men, all like Alex, he sensed—all with the past swirling about them like litter on the street, all with their faces scrubbed and shaved and their hair gelled up or down, all heading onward to the future, believing blindly that what lay ahead must surely rank above what lay sprawled behind.

She recovered, Nan did, the pink wisps of scars around her face like a wreath. The scarring was worse on her arms, where the weltish tissue buckled; and she reported how her breasts and belly were puckered by the purple memory of all those gashes. When she left the hospital, she checked into a psychiatric retreat in North County San Diego, on a former rancho twenty miles in-land from Carlsbad. Alex visited her once, just after he returned from Japan. They sat in wrought-iron rocking chairs on a veranda that overlooked a lemon grove. It was early September, before the start of his senior year, and the rancho's hillside was gold, and in the distance, through the smog, they looked toward the ocean. He was adjusting to being back, and it shocked him how quickly his life in Tokyo, his little life, was receding into the trunk of his past. "It's hard to believe I'm back for good. I miss Japan some-times. A lot, in fact. There was still so much I wanted to do there."

"Like what?"

"I never went to Hokkaido; I just never had the time or money. Other stuff, too."

"Like what?"

"I made a few good friends, but now I wish I'd spent more time with them."

"Like who?"

"I knew a really nice woman named Tamiko who worked in the bookstore near my university. Other people, too." Wind ran through the lemon grove. There on the breeze was the scent of autumn, and just beyond it, or above it, was the powdery scent of Nan, in silk pajamas and a kimono patterned with lily pads that he had bought her at Mitsukoshi. The salesclerk had asked, "For your special lady, yes?"

"Who else did you meet there?"

"This guy named Yosei. He and I sometimes went to the movies together."

"Did you like him?"

"Well, sure," but then Alex realized what she meant. "Not

like that. He was just a friend. Not with Yosei. He's a pal, but not like that."

"Anyone else?" She stared out: Beyond the lemon grove was a swimming pool that was off-limits to the retreat's residents. But someone was swimming in it, bouncing on the diving board. One of the nurses, Nan explained. Her afternoon off. "Isn't there anyone else you want to tell me about?"

He never told his sister about any of the boys and men who passed through his life. They came and went, and he didn't want her to know, didn't want to hear the judgment—or was it something else?—in her voice: *Where'd you meet him? What does he do? How old is he?*

But something had changed, Alex believed. In the quiet of the afternoon, with the sun dazzling the lemons and the swimming pool and burning Alex's arm hanging beyond the veranda's shade, Alex felt certain that his sister had somehow changed. There she was, the knot of her kimono tight, her fist supporting her chin, her hair shorn down like a little boy's. A pensiveness filled her sewn-together face, and Alex barely recognized her.

"During my last month there I met a guy named Jun. I guess I liked him a lot. I suppose you could say we were dating, that we were boyfriends. It's just my luck that my first real boyfriend would live in Tokyo. I met him only four or five weeks before I came home. We met at a coffee shop in Yoyogi, right by my apartment. He asked me if I was from New York because he was going there on vacation. He's a doctor, a young doctor, a gynecologist in fact. Just finished medical school and he was going to New York before he started up his residency. And we spent nearly every day together, during that last month. It was nice. Nicer than I ever thought it could be. I met him on the same day you—" but Alex stopped himself. That detail he shouldn't add.

Instead, maybe he should tell Nan about the time Jun took him hiking on Mount Fuji. About the Buddhist temple in the foothills. He looked to his sister, wondering if she wanted to know more. She had asked, after all. Hadn't she asked? But Nan remained quiet in her rocker; she stared out, surveying the vista, the ranchland, the red tile roofs of the ever-creeping suburb. "Oh, Alex," she said finally. "I don't want to hear about you and your fags."

———

He scratched his key at the lock, and at first it didn't take; Alex realized just then that this was the first time he was returning to his new home. He imagined how familiar this gesture would become—key sliding into slot—and shortly he'd do it without thinking, without any recognition of the turning bolt. His life would become that automatic. But not yet tonight, when the street and the apartment and the handsome heft of Guy still glittered, all part of a dream he hadn't realized he was having. All part of something that had yet to fully take shape. As he entered the apartment a strange wheezing greeted him. At first he thought that a window was open or that a rag was somehow caught over the air-conditioning vent. But the air-conditioning wasn't on, and the windows were closed. The gasping continued, and now Alex heard Guy's voice: "Oh, shit. Oh, shit. Oh, come on, don't do this. Come on, you stupid shit."

It was coming from the kitchen, and when Alex reached the doorway he saw Guy sitting cross-legged in the corner next to the garbage pail. At first he didn't see Alex, and he continued:

"Come on, you stupid cat. Don't do this to me." In his lap lay Joan, croaking for air. Every few seconds her body shook, flopping like a fish on a dock, her head reaching up. And there she was: in Guy's lap, a lap already lodged into Alex's fantasies, the cat that he never thought of as his own, the cat that his sister had left to him, but then Nan hadn't gone anywhere, Saint Joan the cat with a rat trap pressing into her skull. The sweep of the trap's arm had torn through the leathery skin of her ear and lashed out an eye. Blood black as her fur drowned away the expression on her face. It ran over Guy's legs, catching in the hair of his thigh.

Finally he noticed Alex. "She got her head caught in the trap," Guy said, trying—only halfheartedly—to make a joke of it, as if they could laugh it away. And if he could have, Alex would have laughed, too, because surely something about this was funny, but then Alex couldn't think what. Guy stopped, as if the weight of Saint Joan was becoming too much. "I can't get her out."

Alex stood calm. He steeled himself against the pangs that might rise in his chest. He didn't want to become intimate with this crisis; he'd do his best to disallow it. Disasters happen, deaths occur. Skulls are crushed. His sister, when she was twelve, built a playpen for her hamster Ginnie on the porch outside her window. One day, when Alex and the other children in the neighborhood refused to let Nan join their game of sprinkler tag in the backyard, she stormed up to her room and yelled from her open window, "I hope you all die! Every last one of you!" And with that, Nan slammed her window, crushing into its white frame the small bones of the hamster. This story hovered over the family; it was retold often to the pitiful amusement of a large gathering at the dinner table. Oh, how they would laugh at this one now. His mother wiping the corners of her eyes with a monogrammed napkin, and Nan herself giggling about the child she once was. You couldn't help but laugh about it now. But there was another story from that time that wasn't retold. His sister, when she was twelve, one rainy afternoon lay down in the dark hollow of their mother's dressing closet. She had told Alex to enter the blackness after two minutes, and when he did she guided his hands over the soft mounds of her chest. She led his fingers to her warm sticky inside and then made him lick his hand. Alex's heart had stopped at the taste; he felt as if he had taken his last breath.

"I don't understand where it came from," Alex said.

"What?"

"The trap. What was it doing there?"

"I keep one down in that little hole by the dishwasher. Sometimes mice come through it."

"But it's such a big trap. I've never seen a trap that big."

"I once saw a rat. I got a big one just in case."

Alex hadn't asked about rats or mice before he moved in. But why should he have thought to? So much to know about someone before you live with him; so many things you'll never know.

"Can you get it off her?" He squatted next to his roommate, and their knees touched, and Alex felt something like a pilot light spark and try to catch in his chest.

"I'm trying." Guy's voice cracked, approaching panic. "Give me a hand." And then, "Alex, I'm sorry. It never occurred to me . . . I just never thought that she would . . . that you would—" But Guy couldn't finish.

And Alex, too, was slow to move. All he could do was stare

and recall and forget and look ahead. He thought about tomorrow: That was when his new life would start, tomorrow. The empty desk where he'd open his day calendar; the Rolodex he'd begin to fill with typewritten cards; the first telephone call home to Guy to tell him he was running late, he couldn't meet him at the gym. "You'll have to go on without me," Alex imagined himself saying to someone—if not to Guy, then to someone. Yes, tomorrow, after the trap was removed and the body of poor Saint Joan, who just now passed from living to dead, was discarded in the trash bin in the back alley, after that his life, the one he'd been planning his whole life, would begin, and how would it feel to Alex Tuck? How would it feel to this young man, twenty-two, a teetering mass of bone and hurt, to finally feel the catch take hold in his chest, the rise in his throat, and the regrettable burn of coming to life?

REGIME

It is ten o'clock on a Saturday morning, and I am in the boys'
gym, running through a layup drill. A member of the freshman
basketball team, I'm a third-string guard, though sometimes
Coach Lennie scrimmages me as a forward because he still
can't figure out where I'll cause the least damage. An orange
panther is painted in the center of the court, shiny beneath varnish, its tail arched in prowl, and right now I am standing on its
paw, frozen with the fear of prey.

On the court are two lines of boys, and every few seconds Coach Lennie passes a basketball to the boy at the front of the line, who then dribbles it to the basket. Chris Underwood, Tom Heck, Gunnar Janssen—each boy in his orange mesh shorts snatches the ball from the air and begins his drill. The nets are swishing this morning; the team is counting how high we can go before a missed shot. I nervously move closer to the head of the line.

Coach Lennie stands beneath the backboard, the varicose veins in his calves throbbing, sideburns as dense as Velcro. His shorts stretch around his gut and crotch in a way that embarrasses me. I don't like the black hair creeping up his thigh, or those sprouting out of the V neck of his sweater; it makes me think of flypaper and being trapped alive. Coach Lennie puffs on the silver whistle lodged between his lips; I imagine the little gray ball in the whistle whirring around dizzily as Coach Lennie's milky breath blows on it. For some reason my head feels like that gray rubber ball: dizzy and blown-about, a pea-sized bit of foam smudged and damp with saliva. Tom Heck slopes back from his successful layup and says, "Let's go, Jonathan!" A strange purple scar from a bad sunburn glows beneath each of his eyes. The hair between his legs, I have noticed, is platinum. Chris Underwood shuffles back from his drill and says, "Go for it, Jon!" At school he often wears volleyball shorts out of which sometimes peeps a white mound of underwear. Only last July I invited Chris for a sleep-over and for some reason he said yes. He stayed up through the night in the bunk above me, the sag of his blue-and-white mattress somehow feeling like the heavens pressing down, telling me about firecrackers—cherry bombs and bottle rockets and something called the Hungry Hyena. "You ever see one of those, Jon?"

Gunnar Janssen shoves the ball at me. He and I never speak; I understand that he *knows.*

I manage to catch it, with a bit of a fumble, and down the court I move. Each time I lift my foot, my head begins to spin as if I'm short of breath. It's as if I've been running in a circle for a while; hard to take in the proper amount of air. Suddenly the boys' gym dulls over, everything as gray as the whistle's speck of a ball. The basketball slaps against the hardwood floor. On the next bounce it hits my sneaker, but I snag the ball before it can scamper away. I pick up my pace as I approach the free-throw line. Coach Lennie allows me three steps in my layups; otherwise the drill would never progress. The basketball begins to feel heavy. The distance between my hand and the glossy floor grows deeper. The boys' gym begins to vibrate and shrink. With hoots and calls and sneaker screeches, the gym is narrowing into a cave. Something buckles beneath me, and just as I leap forward with the basketball in both hands, just as my feet lift toward the red rim and the silky nylon net, just then the gym goes black—a silent silver-starred black. And this is what I think as my body propels itself up and the world folds itself away: I am completing my first layup in my life. And so it is no surprise when I hear the net swish and feel my body—somehow detached from me— crumple in the air and fall to the floor. Coach Lennie's whistle stills. The world is out. The boys I long for are gone. I am at last alone and everything has disappeared, even me, even my sense of myself—and then I crash against the hardwood floor, my clump of a body reflected in the polyurethane.

When I open my eyes, first I see the boys' knees. Then the white cotton up their shorts. I turn my head and there's the lumpy blue knots in Coach Lennie's leg. Downcourt, Gunnar Janssen is picking at the basketball's seam. Above me, the racks of fluorescent lighting tick, and the Number 14 jersey of a boy, Andy Brown, killed in the fire in the foothills last year, flutters in a draft.

I want to say, "I'm okay," but I can't form the words. I try to pull myself up, but my legs don't move. Someone is saying, "Can he get up? Should I call an ambulance?"

"No," I say.

A couple of the boys cheer.

"Have you been sick?" Coach Lennie asks.

"Not really."

"Hey, Jon! You fainted!" a peppy voice calls. I think I hear someone say, "Cool!"

"I guess I have a cold."

"Help him to the bleachers." Hot hands reach under me and carry me to the sideline. They lay me down, a little less gently than I would like. I manage to say, "Thanks, guys."

"Rest for a bit," Coach Lennie says. His mouth clamps down on the whistle, and the boys reassemble their drill, and I close my eyes and see nothing in my head but the waxy Chap Stick impression Coach Lennie's lips leave on the cold whistle.

I have never fainted before. I have never seen anyone faint. I wonder why this has happened, and at first I believe it must be because of the indignity of playing basketball when I have no skill for it, having to pretend I am one of these Poly Panthers—

long-limbed, tank-topped, proudly counting each new whisker on the chin—when I am not.

Then I recall my little experiment. Today is the third of January. On New Year's Eve I drank six beers and the next day I didn't feel well enough to eat my mother's Rose Bowl chili. In the evening my parents went to a party, and I fed my mother's chicken breast to the dog. Yesterday, still not feeling well, I skipped all meals. Today I woke up with a remote pang in my gut. As I lay in bed I realized my stomach was empty. I began to wonder how long I could last. I asked myself for the first time, How much can you bear?

The day after basketball practice, I feel as though my life has changed. At lunchtime I strategically leave the house just as the orange smell of nachos rises from my mother's microwave. She is smashing an avocado for guacamole; *gwack*, as she calls it. She is wearing a pair of pink shorts, and her thighs tremble as she mashes the yellowing avocado meat with a fork. The fireworks of capillaries in her flesh make me think of Chris Underwood and how he hasn't paid much attention to me in months, except yesterday, as I lay supine on the gym floor. A connection forms, the tingle of understanding. I promise myself I'll never eat again. It is the first time I hate my mother for serving me food.

———

For most of my life I've been the fattest kid in my class. Each September my mother will buy me three pairs of Husky Guy corduroys: tan, blue, and brown. By Christmas the inner thighs will have worn smooth. But not the brown pair. I never wear the brown pair. My mother will apply iron-on patches to the blue and tan cords, but the patches will peel off, exposing my hairless flesh. From Easter to June I will have nothing to wear but the brown pants. *They make you look like a lump of shit*, Marjorie England once said, her ski-jump nose twitching, as she ran to catch up with the boys.

If someone were to ask me about my most prominent feature, I would describe the tube of flesh girdling my waist. Sometimes in junior high I liked my role as the fat kid—shy but occasionally funny, pretty with creamy skin. Sometimes I would trace the tip of a steak knife across my purses of fat. Sometimes I would hold the knife to my penis, pressing as the skin dented white.

A few months before the blackout, my mother took me to Dr. Scull's for a checkup. Dr. Scull wears open golf shirts that shape the hint of his breasts. He is always tan, and something about the way he holds his right hand, as if clutching a glass, makes me think he's most at home poolside, swirling ice in his highball. He has been my doctor since I was born a blue baby, my umbilical cord strangling my throat. During the first few days of my life no one, not even Dr. Scull, could say whether or not the cord had caused permanent damage to my brain. I wheezed in the stainless steel crib, I've been told, exhausted and—as I imagine it now—hurt by such an unpromising start. Yet after a few days I started to show normal signs. Now I always feel as if Dr. Scull holds this against me. At the annual physicals, he is abrupt and uninterested. He laughs loudly at his own jokes and, that once, ignored my small question about the soft hairs between my legs.

This year when I go for my physical, Dr. Scull is the same.

And I am the same: shy, wounded, as if the umbilical cord has been cut from my neck only last night; I am fatter than the last time I stepped on Dr. Scull's scale. In the house there is only one scale, in my mother's bathroom, beneath her flannel nightgown hanging on a hook. For some reason, my sisters tell me never to use it; they say that only girls step onto scales. Boys aren't supposed to care about their weight, my sisters have told me my whole life, even though I am fat and they giggle when my cords wear smooth. Each year Dr. Scull logs into his manila folder my ever-increasing pounds, saying something like, "Let's try to bring this down a bit," or, "Getting up there."

This year after the checkup, I wait for the results with my mother. At moments like this she always looks as if she is about to draw the last fifty dollars from her checking account. She clutches tightly her canvas purse, the kelly green one with her monogram, which she proudly turns outward for others to see. She pats the tips of her grown-out perm. Dr. Scull enters, his hand clinking the imaginary highball. He runs through the report: normal, normal, normal. I sense, yet again, his disappointment in me.

"Now, about your weight," he says, brightening for the first time.

My mother scoots forward, the lines in her forehead suddenly looking like a secret message to Dr. Scull: *I'm going broke feeding him!*

"You're getting fat," he says. And then, "I want you to do me a favor. The next time you want a snack"—Dr. Scull closes the manila file—"grab yourself a carrot instead of a Twinkie."

My mother, who opposes junk food not because of its lack of

nutritional content but because of its price, sits back in her chair, confirmed. The only thing I can feel—for there is no other reality at a moment like this—is the wedge of my stomach pushing with humiliation and sweat against my shirt, the one, although it is outgrown, my mother refuses to retire from my closet. "I can't be buying you a new wardrobe every time you gain ten pounds."

———

Now, January of my freshman year, the week after fainting, I'm at school and Chris Underwood asks, "Hey, Jon, feeling any better?" This is the same boy who has given up on me after I failed to show interest in firecrackers on the fourth of July. Tom Heck says, "That must've sucked. You hit the floor hard, man." Last year Tom invited me for a sleep-over, but because I couldn't stop staring at the little lump in his briefs, like a walnut wrapped in a handkerchief, I never allowed myself to return. Even Gunnar Janssen, who wears his tan corduroys so tight I can see all of him shifting down his right thigh, gives a little smile. Just a smirk. But more than ever before.

For the first time in my life, I have figured out how to draw a boy's interest.

Each morning my mother hands me my lunch in a brown paper bag. I hold it tight in my fist as I ride to school on my ten-speed with the ram's-horn handles. When I arrive on the campus, which is alive with car pools spilling out, I pedal past the garbage can and drop in my lunch. In one fell swoop all those calories fall away. I have enough money for a Diet Coke at noon. I will not eat today. This is part of the game. After four weeks the game is beginning to work. When I hold my hand to the sunlight, it's as if I am looking at the bones through an X ray. That's how I know I am making progress.

In February in French class I learn how to say I'm on a diet: *Je suis un régime.* In my head I translate it this way: I am a regime.

When I am winning the game, I count the hours since I last ate. Twenty-four means nothing. Forty-eight is a start. Seventy-two is when I feel like the most powerful boy in the world. When I haven't eaten for three days I feel, at last, content; I no longer hunger for anything. Instead, I think of myself as a hammered piece of gold, pretty, so thin and airy I could blow away. I feel shiny in the world, as if an impenetrable glow protects me. I take comfort in knowing that I have superseded the daily dirty habits of all mankind—the toilet and the ablutions, the fueling and the purging, the intake and the elimination. On the third day, a tuna sandwich appears poisonous. I'll sit with Marjorie England on the lunch patio and watch her pick at her pita bread, her thumb scooping out the stray globs of tuna left over in the baggie, and I scorn her. I will think: She has no control over her life. I will think: She has sunk to the level of the rest of them.

Without acknowledging it, together Marjorie and I watch the boys: Chris, Tom, Gunnar, the others. They share bags of barbecue potato chips. A bottle of cherry soda moves from one mouth to the next. Powdered doughnuts push past lips; bars of chocolate broken on the tongue; salami staining fingers; milk dripping down the throat. The boys look as if they are out of control, insatiable; animals. They walk up to girls and beg for slices of honey-baked ham. Chris, Tom, and Gunnar would ask Marjorie but they know she will say no. They would ask me, but I don't have any honey-baked ham. I sit, legs crossed, and sip my Diet Coke.

And I think: I have more control over myself than anyone in the world. The third day of self-starvation is the most beautiful day. It is when I believe, at lunch hour, in the shade of a black oak, the brick patio cold beneath my thinning ass: None of you can do what I can, and all of you will like me because of it. It is when the world becomes hyper-bright and I hear everything, I see everything, and I am overcome with a giddy, intoxicating weightlessness. There, with the Pasadena smog a shroud across the sky, I begin to float away.

The fourth day is more difficult. The shimmering intensity of the third day diffuses, replaced by a vague inability to concentrate. It is the day when the world turns gray at the edges, when my vision blurs and it becomes difficult to see clearly across the lunch patio. On the fourth day I no longer feel like a piece of gold but instead a small, dense rock. I have to constantly shift position in my chair because, where others are sitting on muscle and fat, I am—now, thank god—sitting on jutting bone. The bike ride to school leaves me shaking and icy; it is harder and harder to dash between classes. On the fourth day I must steal the quarters from my father's bureau, where he stacks them on a doily, in order to buy a Diet Coke every hour on the hour, inserting the needle of the straw in my mouth and turning on the soda's drip. On the fourth day I have to excuse myself from French class three times to pee. On the fourth day the effort to smile becomes too great. On the fourth day I stumble to basketball practice after school and tell Coach Lennie I'm too sick to play. On the fourth day he permits me to rest on the bench in the boys' gym, or even lie down, and watch Chris and Tom and Gunnar practice their layups and their free throws. It is on the fourth day when one of them, usually Chris, will come up to me and put his hot hand on my knee and say, "Jon, man, is there, like, something really wrong with you?" Sometimes, when I am lying on the bench, he will put a foot up, and I will look with appetite up his shorts. On the fourth day I sit in the locker room with my head in my hands and watch, through my fingers, each of them emerge from the shower. Chris's prick is thick and long and always a bit alive; Tom's is purple at the head; Gunnar Janssen's is perfect, never scrunched up, glistening with a drop of shower water at the tip.

It is usually on the fourth day that I can no longer make excuses about skipping dinner and will have to eat my mother's enchiladas. The food stuffs me like air. It returns a hated energy to me, a nasty will of life. My first feeling after eating is always rage: My mother is trying to kill me by making me eat. The world wants to choke me, forcing food down my throat, and yet still denying me of satisfying my even greater hunger. I sulk at the dinner table, saying nothing. My sisters and my parents chatter around me about the heavy winter rains. They don't notice me slumped in my chair unless the rage rises so strong that I bolt up and take my plate to the kitchen, dropping it sharply on the warped butcher-block counter. A silence explodes back in the dining room. Later my father will knock on my door and say, "Your mother doesn't appreciate it when you. . . ." From downstairs my mother will scream, "Don't throw that enchilada away!"

Like everyone else, my father will fail to notice that I have lost five pounds in this week's regime. He will not see the hollow in my cheek. He ignores my sunken eye. He misses the knobs of my hips pointing out through my cords. I hate him for not noticing me. I am doing this for every man in the world, I believe. I fall asleep, dreaming of a faceless man stripping me and counting the ribs in my chest. He will say, I can't see them all.

———

In March I weigh 120 pounds. This is what I weighed in the fifth grade. I wear baggy sweaters to hide the loss. My mother has always bought my clothes too big, hoping for years of use. She sees me in the morning, a blue cable-knit hanging like a poncho, and I know her only thought is: Thank god I don't have to buy him anything else. She is custardy in the upper arm. She packs my lunch with Dr. Scull's carrot sticks. She begs me to please, please bring back the brown paper bag.

Basketball season has ended. We have come in second-to-last in the league, ahead of Pacific Christian. Their uniforms are black and red and the school is in Eagle Rock, which my mother warns is a dangerous place. "Everyone knows there are gangs there. Everyone's heard about that murder at the ARCO." At that one victorious game against Pacific Christian, because we are ahead, Coach Lennie plays me more than usual. I catch a pass and toss it on. This pass gives Tom an open basket, and I make my first statistic for the season: an assist. Then a player with long arms that are both hard and slick fouls me. This allows me two free throws. The first misses, but respectably. The second—to everyone's astonishment, especially mine—slips past the rim and down the hole of the net. Chris and Tom cheer. Even Gunnar Janssen, whose hair mats down handsomely when he's hot, cracks a smile.

The only reason the basketball has gone in is because the game is on a third day. I am a piece of gold; no one can harm me through the glowing ring of starving gold. Everybody is eating, and I am not. There is one thing that everybody in the world needs that I do not. I have separated myself, and I hug my chest and count my ribs, one, two, three. On the court at Pacific Christian, with my teammates cheering for the first and only point I will ever score, I close my eyes and think about the boys around me; I know they like me because after the game I will race home on my Schwinn and sneak up to my mother's bathroom and pull off my clothes and check the scale to confirm what I already suspect: that through the course of the day—the bicycle ride, the pass on the court, the free throw—I have exerted enough to lose another unforgivable pound.

————

With the basketball season over, Chris and Tom and Gunnar move on to the baseball team. I don't join them. Because my high school believes a healthy body goes hand in hand with a healthy mind, I am required to participate in some sport or other. But now, for the first time, independent sports is an option. My mother signs a form. And so, from March until the end of the school year, I am obliged to work out at the Pasadena Athletic Club three times a week. I am entrusted to sweat alone.

The Pasadena Athletic Club is on Walnut Street in a poured concrete building with sunbathing terraces on every floor. There are three tennis courts on the roof of the parking garage, and a mirrored weight room. On my first day, a man named Joey shows me through the Nautilus equipment, his nylon pants rubbing noisily as we move from the lateral press to the thigh curl, and back. He is a little shorter than me but has nicely muscled arms and a throat with two thumping arteries. Each morning, I imagine, he applies a palmful of gel to his hair, spiking it up. He refuses to look at me as he explains how to work the butterfly machine. Right away I know that I bore him. His upper lip, which is full and beautifully pink and greasy with balm, curls in disdain. He wears a gold necklace that hangs snugly around his throat, and all I can wonder about, instead of the thigh curl or the butterfly, is who—yes, who?—gave him the gold necklace. On what occasion does Joey take it off?

After my first workout, Joey says, "You've seen the locker room?" He leads me to the first floor, down a hall with beige tiles and the chlorine smell of swimming pool. There is a doorway with wooden saloon doors on hinges. Joey shoves his way through. "Towels over here. Lockers down there." We step into a tiled area where there is a man in a white towel with one yellow stripe shaving at the sink. "Showers down around that corner," Joey says. "And that's the sauna. And over there's the steam."

Joey's hand falls on my back. Today is a second day, which usually means very little, but now I am feeling dizzy. The tiled room seems to be dimming. I can feel the sweat blooming on the small of my back, on my sternum, between my legs. "Take it easy, kid," Joey says. He leaves me.

I am standing near the sink where the man is shaving. He is wet, but I can tell it is wet not from showering but from sweat. He is also tall, and his stomach is hairy. He wears blue plastic sandals. His narrow face is red from the razor. His eyes are gray and in the mirror they meet mine. Then they jump away.

Down one of the aisles of lockers I pull off my clothes. I wrap myself in a towel. It is difficult to get the towel to hold around my waist, because I do not have a waist. I only have a concave bowl of skin around my belly button and two points of hipbone, as blunt as doorknobs. I shawl myself up in a second towel. I clutch a third in my fists. I am afraid that someone might see my flesh. Other than my legs, I do not want anyone ever to see my flesh. I know for a fact that it is too grotesque to reveal. I know that, despite the starvation, an unpleasant softness remains in my skin. I am my mother's son, with her doughy breasts, with her padded hips. I am a fat child. I will always remain a fat child.

When I open the door to the steam room, a hot wet cloud rolls in my face. Inside it is yellowy dark. The air smells of eucalyptus, and at first it is hard to breathe. I stand at the door, my eyes adjusting. There is a machine at the opposite end of the room coughing out the steam. After a few seconds I make out that there are two benches facing each other. Although I cannot see for sure, something tells me that someone is sitting on one of them. I sit on the opposite, feeling my way over the drippy tiles. I settle back, blanketing the third towel across my stomach.

Very quickly I like the wet dark air. I close my eyes. I begin to slip into the calm, floating feeling of a third day—the third day a day early. When my eyes are shut, I see gold. I can see myself sitting on that slippery bench with the steam surrounding me. It's as if my brittle husk of a body is there in the steam room but I am somewhere else.

No one can ever touch me.

Because I am not here.

I am at the point where the body is separated from the soul. It makes me think of my mother's steak knife—the flat blade shaving away pounds of flesh from a thigh, a belly, a groin. Scraping until bone. It is all I will need in life: myself and my bones.

The machine stops coughing. The shadowy room becomes quiet. Drops fall from the ceiling. The dark figure shifts on the bench across from me. He is all gray, and the only thing that I can tell about him is that he is tall. Every minute or so he shifts, scratching the heel of his foot or stretching with a yawn. Some of the steam clears, and I can tell he has a hairy chest and bony knees. But his middle is strangely hidden beneath a veil of steam. More minutes pass and then I can see he is the man from the sink. There are a few spots of shaving cream on his chin. His face is even redder from the heat, and a drop of sweat hangs from his nose. Now his eyes are dark. His Adam's apple is a fast-moving blade. One of his hands rubs the sweat into his chest. My eyes fall to his lap, but the steam lingers there. I look to the ceiling, where there is a lozenge-shaped lamp that casts the dull yellow light. The way the moisture hangs in drops from the lamp makes me think of the sweat on the tip of the man's nose, and when I look back to him, much of the steam has disappeared. And there he is: directly across from me, his body red and damp, his knees pointing out, his towel split open, and his penis standing alert and pink. On its tip glistens a drop of something wet.

And I leave.

———

After that I ride my bike to the Pasadena Athletic Club five or six times a week. My workouts are hard but I do not want to build muscle; no, I want to burn flesh. Sometimes I set out for a run from the club. My old basketball shoes carry me down into the

Arroyo Seco and around the parking lots of the Rose Bowl, past the golf course and the Rose City Lounge. I will run for an hour, and I'll feel like a ship at sea, as if, were something to go wrong, help would not come easily. I run hard, and there is nothing I like more than to return to the Pasadena Athletic Club and in the long mirror see the splattered mud on my legs, which thin with each passing week. A calf and thigh that are my own creation; a sharp ankle bone.

After each run, I enter the steam room hopefully. But the man, whom I've begun calling the Pink Man, never reappears. And no one similar replaces him. Every now and then a handsome man with a chest swollen from bench-pressing will saunter into the steam. I will sit up and adjust the knots of my soggy towels, but these men usually close their eyes and pay me no attention. I study their bodies carefully, the way the hairs crawl out of their belly buttons, or the shade of their beards. It's at moments like this when I feel especially hungry, but it's also when I know that were I to feast, whether on the man ignoring me in the steam or on the tortilla chips and *gwack* that my mother shoves out in a ceramic bowl, my life would end.

Or at least: Something in my life would end. I would lose myself in the rest of the world.

———

One day, after a workout, I am rushing down the stairs to the locker room. I do not feel well, because last night my mother made me eat her hamburger. The pale oily meat clutters my stomach. But my mother has begun to suspect that something is wrong with me. She has asked, "Are you hiding something?" I hope she thinks I'm on drugs. She has become more mindful of my habits at dinnertime. She carefully watches the bulge of food creep down my throat. Lately my sisters have been calling me Mr. Concentration Camp, their voices screeching with envy. I hate them for one reason: They are trying to ruin the most miraculous thing I already know I will ever do in my life: To live without sustenance. To live on nothing more than the fuel of my soul.

But on this day at the Pasadena Athletic Club, a boy my age stops me on the stairwell. "Don't I know you from someplace?" He is tall and is wearing a tank top and there is a meatiness to his shoulder. A basketball is lodged beneath his arm.

"I don't think so."

"Well, where do you go to school?"

"Poly."

"That's it." He snaps his fingers. "We played you last season. I go to Pacific Christian. You guys beat us, remember?"

I nod.

"I remember you," he says. "You were a pretty good player."

"That wasn't me."

"No, I remember you. You were, like, passing the ball around all the time. Setting up points and stuff."

"You must be thinking of someone else."

"No, man. It was you. Don't you remember? I fouled you. And you made your second free throw." He pantomimes a shot.

The boy's name turns out to be Albert, and he invites me to the racquetball lounge, where he buys me an iced tea. We sit in vinyl swivel chairs while Albert talks about basketball and Pacific Christian and how much he hates it there. He also says he hates his mom, who is a psychologist, and his little sister, who has a vague disorder of the lung. "I wish I could go to Poly," he says. This startles me because no one has ever said to me that he wishes for anything from my life.

The iced tea quickly makes me nervous. Soon I say I must go.

"But let's shoot some hoops sometime," Albert says.

"I still don't think you remember me correctly. I can't play basketball."

"Would you shut up with that." He smiles and pats the basketball between his thighs. "If you can't play, I'll teach ya."

———

The next week I am in the workout room lying on my stomach, whipping my way through a set of thigh curls. Today is a third day. When I look up, there is Albert rubbing his basketball. He asks me to meet him on the court. I say I can't. He takes my wrist and gives me a little tug.

On the echoey court, Albert runs through a layup and then passes the ball to me. But for the first time in my life I am not embarrassed when I say, "I don't like to play."

Albert walks to me. He sets down the basketball and then pokes me gently in the breast. "These are the steps." Slowly he leads me through the paces of a layup, my pipe of a wrist in his hand. I follow him, step step step, and then the little half jump. Albert holds my hand up, and together we pass an imaginary basketball into the net.

Albert and I meet on the basketball court a couple of times a week. He is always there before me, horsing around by himself. I like to watch him through the window in the gym door as he dribbles in boredom. His hair is a dark blond, and his nose makes me think of a nibbling rabbit. He is nearly hairless, except for a few fine gold wisps beneath his arms and, I assume, down there. His tank top shows off the flank of his chest. Inside his baggy gym shorts his cock dangles about like a wind chime.

After playing on the basketball court, where I am beginning to learn to make a shot or two, we'll drink iced tea in the racquetball lounge. Eventually Albert will say, "Let's head to the showers." But I always decline. I know I cannot shower with Albert. I know I cannot expose my crude body with its colorless skin and protruding bones. I know I cannot stand beneath a showerhead next to Albert's naked body without hungrily kneeling down.

———

I have stalled out at 110 pounds. My mother has set down some rules about attendance at meals. When she and my father aren't there to watch me eat, she sics my sisters on me. She begins to ask directly whether or not I have eaten the lunch she packed. Sometimes I lie, sometimes I refuse to answer at all. I have set my sights on 105 pounds. After several months of monitoring the cycles of food moving through me, I have figured out that 105 pounds is the cusp where I want to live.

One evening Albert meets me at the club. My parents are away at a conference in Atlanta and so I am having a third day. Albert and I play basketball. It is late, and for the most part the club is empty. We decide to walk through the racquetball courts, where kids aren't allowed. This makes me nervous, but Albert says, "Come on." There is a long hallway with small white doors on either side. I have never been in here, and there is a silence to the place that rings in my ears. We enter the last door. The court is white but smudged. The lights are bright overhead. Everything echoes, even the weak panting of my breath.

Albert pulls a blue rubber ball from his shorts. He begins

tossing it against the wall, catching it, hurling it again. He tells me to catch it, but I miss and have to chase it across the floor. He tells me to throw it, and I do: a soft arcing lob that barely hits the far wall.

"You throw like a girl," Albert says, smiling. He gently pushes my shoulder. Something tells me he means it as a compliment.

"Shut up."

"Make me." He shoves me again, and yet I am not hurt by this shove. I am brought to the hyper-alertness of a third day. The way his long fingers fall around the bone of my shoulder; the force of energy hurtling down his bicep, across his wrist, through his fingers, and into me; the way his eyes widen as my body absorbs his shove; the way his buckteeth emerge from beneath his lip to form the nibbling-rabbit face.

Albert moves close to me, so close to me that I can smell his wet-leaf odor and see the pores in his nose. He is releasing a dull warmth. He is standing in front of me, a thin space between us, and then I notice the lump in his shorts; it is pointing upward, aimed at me. It juts out, practically touching the hem of my T-shirt. Albert says nothing. I say nothing. I am frightened, and I am feeling more light-headed than before. Just tonight the scale in the locker room tipped to the correct side of 110 pounds for the first time. I assume that only I, and not Albert, want to feast, and that Albert does not share my hunger. It does not occur to me that this is a mutual longing. This is a trap, and if I were to step into it I would be caught forever: I would become a devouring fiend for the rest of my life.

I leave the racquetball court. I mumble, "See you later." Albert hurls the blue rubber ball against the wall.

With my parents in Atlanta, I do not need to go home. It is now almost ten o'clock on a Friday night. The locker room is quiet; a lone metal *slam!* comes from another aisle. I yank off my clothes, hopping clumsily out of my underpants. Three towels I knot around myself. The only thing I can think to do is to escape to the steam. To hide from Albert in the steam.

When I open the door, the old wet cloud greets me. One of the bulbs in the lamp has burned out and the room is dimmer than usual. I sit on one of the benches, tucking my towel knots. As the steam hisses, I close my eyes and wait until I can feel my pores opening. This is how it will be: my bony self in a cloud of steam, hiding from what I crave. My clavicle feels like a coat hanger, my tailbone the knob of a locked kitchen cupboard. I am a regime.

When the steam machine hacks to a stop, at first I hear nothing, but then a sigh emerges in the room. The steam is shifting, and a dark image appears on the bench opposite me. I can see nothing but the dark pile of a faceless man. He sighs again, and then there's a wet slapping sound of his hand wiping away sweat. I wish the man were Albert. Then I think he might be Albert, his tall dark shape seeming familiar. I can't be sure, but the long legs suggest my new friend from Pacific Christian, and then I realize that here in the dark weepy room we can meet without really seeing each other. Albert and I will hold each other blindly. The steam will become our bedclothes, our comforter. It is Albert, I tell myself. He has come.

I wonder what I am supposed to do next. Will my flimsy sense of restraint fall away? Fall as my body becomes damp from the steam and the sweat, which is running into my eyes with a sting?

I seal my eyelids, and the machine begins to chortle again, sputtering out a few new clouds. It clanks like an old radiator. I press my palms against my lids until all I can see is a dark gold sea. Today is a third day, but it's starting to feel like a fifth, which are the days I am in so much pain that all I really long for is to die.

A minute passes, maybe longer, and when I open my eyes something is in front of me, and in the fastest second of my life I understand everything. The man is not Albert but the Pink Man. He has found me and is standing at my bench, his stomach hairy and wet, his eyes gray, his cock hard in his fist. The Pink Man is jacking off in my face, and I become stuck to the tile bench. I cannot move, my blood is watered-down fuel; I cannot run away or shove him back to his bench, cannot lift my hand, which lies heavily on my thigh, not even to shield my face from the man or to touch my prick, which strains against my towel. No, I sit and stare at the blue head of his cock. I watch his grip slide up and down and the way he arches himself up on the balls of his feet. I listen to the sloshing sound, the quick breath, the muttered words that sound like *Fuck you, fuck you.*

I can do nothing but look ahead, at the eye of his cock. I watch and wait, and feel myself both present and already drifting away, gone, a grimy feather in a downdraft. Earlier, I didn't want to touch Albert's dick because I knew that, with that one reach of the hand, I would lose control. I don't want to touch any cock because it is a slippery slope, like a sack of barbecue potato chips, and I have come to fear a bag of chips greater than I fear myself. Oh, in life: Who can sample just one? Sex will be like that, like life itself, and not only will it drag me down into a perpetual state of craving but so will nourishing myself, clamping my lips around something hard and greasy that will leave an aftertaste on my tongue, on my sterile breath. Right now I am a special boy, and I want to always remain a special boy, but the man's fist is moving faster. It is so close to my face that I wonder if it will fly out and punch me in the mouth, which I then realize is gaping open. The man is beginning to groan, he is beginning to say *suck it,* his cock looks especially red and fierce, and just as he leans forward, his free hand propping himself against the wall, the Pink Man explodes. A teaspoon of his seed lands on my tongue. It is my first meal in three days, in three weeks, in three months, and as its saltiness slides down my throat as my stomach begins to churn on this long-delayed nourishment, I know that now and forever I will remain hungry, hunting for food, hunting for men, sated for only hours at a time, perpetually seeking more.

THE ROSE CITY

On an October morning not long ago, Roland Dott—six willowy feet, his nose shaped by surgery—drove to the Pasadena Athletic Club, squinting against the glare. He was annoyed with himself because he had that feeling that he'd forgotten to do something although he couldn't think what. It was Friday, nothing jotted in the agenda except the aerobics class and a date with Michael to hit out a bucket of balls. So what else could he have forgotten to do?

In the men's locker room Roland undressed and stood in front of the mirror. He kept his locker down a side aisle, where traffic was light; this allowed him to look at himself as long as necessary. Last time he was here, he was plucking the hairs from his nose when two men, sweaty from the squash courts, came upon him, his nostril turned inside out. "I think you missed one," the first man said. The second laughed. The men slapped each other's damp backs and then collapsed onto the bench, hauling their fungal feet out of their stinky sneaks: *Better off dead than smell like that,* and in the pot of his chest Roland, who was forty-eight but you wouldn't know it, boiled a batch of distaste, one that would stay with him through the day.

But it was a Friday morning, meaning the type of men who sweat on the squash court were at the office, dampening their stay-stiff collars and the crotch of their khakis. Roland continued pushing the tweezers at the silver-white lining of his nostril, wondering if he'd forgotten to turn off his hot plate, but he hadn't turned it on; it'd been a while since he'd turned on the hot plate. No, that wasn't it. And he hadn't forgotten to beat back the bush because he was doing that just now—plucking the patch of hairs between his brows. And the strays that sprouted around his nipples. Pretty nipples, he'd been told over the years. Pretty the way the pendant of jade dangled between them. "Blessed with good genes," someone had once said about Roland Dott.

And so maybe on this Friday morning in October he hadn't forgotten anything at all.

He first joined the club years ago, before it moved into its new concrete building on Walnut Street, when he still went by the name of Rol (sounds like a *roll* of mints). There was a boy in his class at John Muir High, Tommy Linda, who used to call him that. *Watcha doing after the game, Rol?* Tommy Linda would ask, giving his fly a hitch. *Oh you know, Tommy. This and that.* He was always too embarrassed to call Tommy Linda *Linda* even though that's what everyone at school called him. *Linda.* With his sandy hair oily at the tips and his sneaks squeaking against the linoleum tiles in Western Civ and his habit of picking at the tunnel of his ear. Linda, whom every girl at John Muir High wanted to date, or to be more precise, screw; whom many girls—as Roland overheard through the aluminum air vent that connected the boys' locker room to the girls'—already had.

Pluck, pluck, pluck, and now Roland knew he was a different man. He brushed his hair down over his forehead in that way he'd read about in the magazine that fell out of Michael's bag the last time they'd met at the driving range. Good old Michael, within the hour he'd be buying the two of them a bucket of balls and then perhaps a bite. Not that Michael would notice the freshly plucked nose or the fashionably tousled hair. *But that's the point;* beauty's in the details, Roland told himself often, wondering who had said it first, and then eventually forgetting that anyone had said it before him. *Well, you know what I've come to discover,* more than once Roland had been heard mumbling, usually late in the night before a last call. *I've come to discover that beauty's in the details.* Had he ever said it to Michael? He hoped not; how he hated to think he'd repeated himself while they practiced their golf swings. That was something Michael would do. Like the way he'd say from time to time, "You know, it feels like I've known you a long time, Roland. Over the years Graham used to talk about you quite a bit." Poor Michael, forgetting what he said, and to whom.

It was a little more than a year ago when Michael had spotted Roland filling his tank at the ARCO on Lake Avenue. "Is your name Roland Dott?" He startled Roland, his fingers falling on Roland's arm at the pump. A clumsy explanation followed, with gasoline fumes swirling in their nostrils: Michael mentioning Graham, saying he was Graham's, well, what was the term? He was Graham's survivor, his widower really; Graham and he had lived together for seventeen years, and now that Graham's gone his memories are somehow becoming my own, and over the years he kept talking about you, Roland, he'd show me pictures, and now, here you are.

They'd gone for a walk on the Cal Tech campus, kicking the jacaranda blossoms littering the path; they'd stopped for a cinnamon coffee in a narrow shop that once housed Huggins' Shoes. Roland had spilled his coffee in Michael's lap, and there was an awkward moment of helping dab at the stain. Each avoided talking about his years with Graham; instead, they both carefully shared details about their pasts. Roland alluded to a setback or two: A few years ago he had checked into a fat farm outside Cathedral City when things weren't good for him. Last year he'd lost his father's signet ring in a burglary. "How'd the burglar get into your apartment?"

"Well, I had no idea he was a burglar when I—" but Roland stopped, realizing that Michael didn't know what he was talking about. It was a question like that that could remind you why

Roland and Graham had called it the quits so many years ago, why Graham had always been meant to end up with someone like Michael.

Something Roland liked to remind people of was his status as a native of Pasadena, born and raised. "Pasadena is where California's real history is, where its real class is," he'd say, to Michael or the boy who sold the bucket of balls or his aerobics instructor or the men he chatted up in the locker room. "But you don't meet many of us natives. We're something of a rarity. Most of this town is made up of trannies." "Of *what*?" "Of transplants. But not my family. We go back. *Way* back, to last century, maybe even further. Records get sketchy before then." Roland would study the eyes of his listener; he who failed to understand the importance of this heritage, well, Roland had no time for him. "My family's as much a part of the history of this town as anyone else. The name Dott means something around here," though if you were to ask you'd find that he based this on something less than evidence. "But that's beside the point," Roland would declare, about all sorts of inquiries, with a wave of the hand. It was beside the point that they had arrested his father for hijacking a float, a Duesenberg draped in delphiniums, during the 1952 Rose Bowl Parade; it was beside the point that his mother used to work the orange groves, and I don't mean climbing the trees to shake down the fruit. No, she was what was once known as a ranch hand's hand. But all that was beside the point because it was years ago, and isn't it funny how history capably changes itself over time?

Roland lived above a garage on Grand Avenue on the estate of an entertainment lawyer. The little two-roomer, rented for a steal, had a pitched ceiling and hand-crank windows that rattled nervously when the Santa Anas blew. There wasn't a proper kitchen, only the hot plate and a waist-high refrigerator, but that was all Roland needed. Someplace to keep his Slim-Fast shakes and his bag of ice, and a carton of orange juice should he need a mixer on the fly. He'd lived there for a while now—how long was it? A few years, but if Roland were to stop and count the time he'd discover he had occupied the garage apartment for nearly a decade. The wife of the lawyer was named Holly, and she liked to entertain during the day while the lawyer was in Studio City shouting into his phone and studying the pie charts of his brokerage account on the computer screen and while their daughter was at the prep school on California Boulevard. Over the years Roland had lost count of the men who had passed through Holly's kitchen door, the cat-flap swinging in their wake: the delivery boy from the florist pulling up the drive in his white station wagon with the decals of tulips on the side panel; the lawyer's best friend, a lanky pink man always biting his lip; the lawyer's client, an Italian producer, bloated in the throat; the gym coach from the prep school, a short man with out-of-date sideburns who made a few extra bucks teaching the teenagers of Pasadena how to drive. And a few women, too, passed through the kitchen door, but oh god, Roland didn't want to think about that; he tried his best to look the other way when the cat-flap went swinging. Holly had a weight problem, hauling around an extra fifteen pounds, and sometimes she and Roland chatted in the driveway about that cruel monster Scotty the Scale, the way naughty Scotty would spin out bad news as if on cue. He'd sometimes hear Holly rummaging in the garage for something, for some sort of tool, and to tell the truth Roland didn't know what she needed a power drill for in the middle of the day. To tell the truth, he knew far more than he wanted to about the lawyer's family—trannies, though they pretended otherwise—but not once did it occur to Roland that they knew even more about him.

The estate wasn't far from the club on Walnut, or from Pasadena's downtown, which a few years back people started calling Old Town, now that a group of concerned ladies had revitalized it, kicking out the pawnshops and the peep shows, luring in the stores that specialized in casual Friday khakis and wedding registries. And in the other direction, to the west, was the Arroyo Seco, a canyon cradling the Rose Bowl, where Roland in his youth spent more than a few football games shredding tickets in half and, later, after the final touchdown, giving the far corner of the parking lot a circle or two. After all, you never know where he's going to turn up; might as well be the Z section of the Rose Bowl parking lot; might as well be beneath your well-plucked nose. Who, you're asking? Who might turn up? Well, if you have to ask, you've never met Roland Dott. You've never had to hunt for life like Roland Dott.

And beyond the Rose Bowl was the public golf course, eighteen holes and a driving range, with a Tahitian-style clubhouse called the Rose City Lounge. Sometimes after a bucket he and Michael would stop by for a drink and a trip to the salad bar. It was a nice enough place. True, the booths could stand a re-upholstering and the help, as Roland liked to point out, could turn snappy over something as harmless as a spilled Manhattan, but the salad bar had a diet Thousand Island that Roland—

he told Michael every time they went for lunch—could die for. When the weather wasn't too hot and the smog level was low, a pair of glass doors opened to a patio that overlooked the parking lot, and out there Roland could monitor who was stopping by the driving range: the salesman doughy in the sack of his knit shirt, the teenager cockily waving a Big Bertha, the lady in the pink visor clamping her lips around a last smoke before heading home to the kids. Once, from the Rose City's patio, he'd witnessed a vandal, a kid with a knife slashing the tires of a minivan with a toy poodle bopping around inside, and Roland liked to recount the way he'd shouted from his chair, "You're scaring the dog."

"Graham used to say you were such a brave man," Michael had said, once or twice, in that silly way of his. "Now I see why."

———

Back from his aerobics class, Roland stood flushed in front of the mirror. He liked the way a good chug of the heart brought color to his cheek, and he hoped it would remain until he met up with Michael down at the Rose City. But there was something Roland was supposed to do between now and meeting Michael, and still he had no idea what it was. Sometimes certain hunches take hold of you, and it turns out the hunches are incorrect. Hadn't Roland lived long enough to know that could be the case? Some days you live in fear of not doing what you were meant to, and the truth of the matter is there's nothing you were meant to do; or so Roland thought, placing the jade pendant between his lips and sucking on it mindlessly. A man in a pair of bicycle shorts passed Roland, everything on display in a cheap sort of way, and Roland regretted that they'd admit anyone to the club these days, any old one prepared to pay his dues. It didn't used to be like that; the old club required an interview and a letter of reference, or preferably a legacy of Pasadena blood, of which Roland possessed ample supply.

The poured concrete of the Pasadena Athletic Club on Walnut was a stark contrast to the club's old Beaux Arts building that once sat proudly on Colorado Boulevard between the equally grand Civic Center and the 1926 city library. Roland had been a member of the club for years, and he missed the way things used to be, with the potted-palm entry and the echoey indoor pool that every morning had special hours for swimming in the nude. A wrecking ball had smashed through the old club's Spanish-tile roof about the time Roland and Graham were winding down. Down came the club, and several blocks with it, clearing the way for the Pasadena Plaza, a shopping mall built of beige brick, anchored by a JCPenney where a few years ago a woman murdered her sister in the changing room; fighting over a pantsuit, 40 percent off, according to the *Star-News*. Trannies, the newspaper reported, but what can you expect?

The new club wasn't as elegant and the hours for swimming in the nude had gone with the wrecking ball, but it was more up-to-date, with a mirrored aerobics studio and plenty of terraces for sunbathing. But Roland missed the style of the old club, the oak lockers and the attendant in the white coat named Leonardo; for a short while he and Graham had shared the key to Number 147, an upper locker with a shelf for their shaving cream and their comb. They stood across the street, their shoulders touching, to watch the silvery-black mass of the ball punch through the granite walls and the red tile roof; they held each other as the chimney fell. "We'll miss it, won't we, Rol?" Graham had said at the time.

As he toweled himself down, Roland thought: In half an hour Michael would be pulling his golf clubs from the trunk of his car. He was tall, thick in the arms and legs, in the throat, but not fat; he spoke sluggishly in a way that might make you think he was slow in the head, but that wasn't true. You could mistake him for a lug, as Roland first had; you might think Michael was the type of man who couldn't keep himself on time, but that wasn't true either, and now Roland checked his watch. He had enough time for a quick steam: He'd have to be fast, but the steam was important because it was the only thing that could clean out his pores.

"I thought only lesbians played golf." That's what Roland had said when Michael phoned after the walk through Cal Tech with an invitation to hit out a few balls. "What on earth would I do at a driving range?" But then Roland stopped to consider who else might be practicing his swing—businessmen with elbows lubricated by gin, the caddies in their baggy shorts. Of course Graham had loved to play golf as well, not that he ever managed to drag Roland down to the links. Years ago—*God, how many?*—Roland and Graham had lived together for a year and a half. Don't ask Roland for a precise date, but it was probably 1972, long before it was simply one more thing the world had gotten used to. Roland had invented a hyphenation: Roland Paires-Dott. Not much of a tongue-roller, so you can understand why he dropped the Paires when it was over.

Roland left the steam room, clearing out of the way of a college kid who wanted to sprawl out. It had been Roland's first night as a waiter at the Valley Hunt Club when they'd met all those years ago. He'd led Graham and his mother and his little brother Kenny to a table out by the swimming pool. The burgundy velvet uniform had fit Roland well, with its jacket cropped snugly at the waist. Roland made a point of dropping their menus and bending to pick them up. It was a little cheap, this move, but it reeled Graham back to the Valley Hunt Club the next night, this time alone, for a grilled tongue sandwich at the bachelor's bar in the Hunt Room. "Gosh, we couldn't be more different, but I like that about you, Rol," Graham had said when they went for their first drink at the Miyako Inn— Roland's suggestion. Over the years he had learned that the Miyako's kimono ladies didn't care who Roland drank sake with, or how much he stroked the hand of his date; they would pour and cluck and present a dish of quartered oranges and the bill in a blue porcelain bowl. It might all sound quaint now, but listen, boys, not so long ago the world was like this and the Miyako Inn was the only place in Pasadena for you and me.

When they went for the walk around Cal Tech, Michael had gone on about the way Graham used to say Roland had taught him things. "He used to say you were the one who first told him to stand up for who he was," Michael had said, but Roland had no idea what he was talking about. "In the last few years Graham said a couple of times he hoped to run into you, Roland. He assumed he would one day."

"Sooner or later you run into everyone in Pasadena," Roland added, taking comfort in the knowledge that Graham's memories had remained fond.

"I can see why he fell for you," Michael tossed out, once or twice, with a bit of plea in his lip. "He would talk about your eyes." Used to call them sapphires, Roland recalled, and all this talk reassured him that they hadn't dulled over into middle age. Roland had taken to frosting his bangs, a trick for washing out the gray. One day when Michael reached out and playfully messed with Roland's hair, in a way that Linda used to do back at John Muir High, Roland felt relief, knowing that the frosted tips had done the trick. A few weeks ago at the driving range Michael had asked, "Have you been ill? There's a thinness to you." But Michael, solid as a black oak, would never understand that two pounds could bulk Roland up and hang like sandbags from his hips. "I've got to be careful. I've got to watch out for naughty Scotty. Take a look at Holly."

Holly who? Scotty what?, but Roland realized it wasn't worth the trouble to explain. Last night the voices of Holly and the lawyer had risen in argument, punctuated by a hurled dinner plate, every word traveling through the cat-flap and across Roland's windowsill. They were fighting over a bill from a mail-order catalog. Seven hundred dollars' worth of underwear. "But it's hand-sewn in Milan! Made of Como silk!" The poor lawyer, would he ever catch on?

Good old Michael, he managed to keep up top a full head of hair, dingy blond and parted down the middle, silver in the side-burns. He was handsome, more handsome than Graham ever was, built like a heaped tower of muscle, and oddly hairless. It made Roland think of a stack of old tires, their tread worn bald. No, Graham had been lean in a high-school-basketball-star sort of way, neither bony nor beefy, a fine enough body though always a bit inept and coltish. When they had lived together, Roland would tease Graham about his pegged trousers and his narrow ties, about his inclination to wear a sports coat to dinner, even at the Salt Shaker; it was the native in him. Michael—a trannie but Roland never brought it up—stayed current with fashions, showing up at the driving range in ironed khakis and casual Friday shirts and a silver tank watch. He was a marketing executive in charge of the doll division of a toy company in Arcadia; he told Roland that his latest toy was in those television commercials with the doll touring the White House. Roland knew Michael liked to talk about his job; and Roland felt it his duty to listen, to a point. Michael was one of those guys the world thinks it can count on, and the world is right. When the president of the toy company went into labor in her office, who do you think was there with a sterile sheet? When the Whittier earthquake rattled Pasadena, who do you think organized the food drive? When Roland needed a ride to visit his mother in the home down in Carlsbad, it was Michael who offered, arriving at the garage apartment with a begonia wrapped in yellow foil.

During the past year they'd had some good times, Roland and Michael. "We're a funny pair," Michael said the first time he took Roland to the golf course.

"We are?"

"Funny in a good sort of way. You know, the Odd Couple."

"That's what Linda used to say."

It's what Graham used to say as well, holding Roland protectively, telling him crazy things like he'd never love another man. Oh, and Roland had forgotten this one: Graham used to beg for

Roland to tell him that he'd never loved anyone more than him. "But what about Linda?" Roland had once said, thoughtlessly. "I'm pretty sure I loved him more." You can imagine how this tore up old Graham, so Roland tried again: "But only in that teenage sort of way. That doesn't count, does it, Graham? I was seventeen."

They didn't know each other, Graham and Linda. Yet so much alike. High-school boys they'd always remain, at least in Roland's eyes, living in the same part of his memory; and in some ways they had become a single memory. Mama's boys, each would melt when his mother padded into the room. Both had liked it when Roland would sink his chin into his fist and say, "Go on. And then what'd you do?" They shared a love of golf. They never knew each other, of course. Years ago Roland had told Graham about Linda. But Linda never heard anything about Graham. How could he? Sniper fire through the heart, on the bank of the Perfume River downstream from Hue. Moldy in a military casket before nineteen. Oh, that was a day for Roland, when he read it in the *Star-News*. They hadn't spoken in more than a year, but that was a day. No, Graham never knew Linda.

And now here Roland was with Michael, who a little over a year ago had had his own day, too. Not long after Roland and Graham had called it the quits, Michael came into the picture. The details had reached Roland's ear through gossip: a Seville-style house, an all-white rose garden, two Jack Russells digging up the winter rye, Buckingham and Kensington they were called. Seventeen years together, and Graham and Michael started thinking about adopting a Russian baby, even wallpapered the guest room like a nursery, but then one day Graham had dropped dead, just like that. And it wasn't the dim-grim A, if that's what you're thinking. No, it was much simpler than all that: One morning Graham's old heart rang up and called it the quits.

Oh yes, it must have been a day for Michael, finding Graham slumped on the patio chaise, his pale skin burning in the morning sun; but it was a less than gorgeous day for Roland, too, opening the *Star-News* and getting a look at poor Graham's obit. That was how Roland had found out. What a day, and now here they were, Roland and Michael, a pair of golf buddies, a couple of men missing a mutual friend, and who would have pictured it? Not Roland, back at old John Muir High.

———

Showered and dressed, Roland exited the club. The sun had broiled the vinyl in his car, and he had to spread a damp towel across the seat. Before he pulled out of the parking lot, he checked himself in the rearview: hair in place, cheek pink, gold chain laying prettily around his throat. He touched the piece of jade. The car didn't have A.C., so he'd have to drive with the windows rolled down, and he worried he hadn't sprayed his hair enough to keep its hold in the draft; Roland would have to drive slowly. He liked to look good for Michael, knew it was something Michael took pride in, meeting someone as kept-up as Roland. Some men have so little to look forward to, and Roland didn't mind doing his part. Yes, Roland had always done his part for so many men.

Linda, then Graham, and now this Michael. But Michael was different. And the others in between. Like a monkey swinging from the vine of one man to the next, but Roland didn't think of himself as a monkey. He was too diligent about beating back the bush. It's what his mother used to call him when he was little. "Come sit in my lap, you little monkey," and Roland would re-sist, getting her to beg, and only then would he comply. It was a trick he'd learned early; a ploy that worked even today.

And the funny thing was, Roland thought as he wheeled the car toward the Rose City: The funny thing was, in some ways, everything he knew had come from her. "If he wants me, he's going to have send more than a box of See's," she'd say, as she headed out to her night shift, sniffing the candy. "A pound of chocolate doesn't buy you a girl these days, oh, no, not anymore. Take it from me, Monkey, this guy's no hubby-hub. Let's you and me forget about him." Of course her years as a hand's hand had taken place when she was a teenager, when orange groves still blossomed in Pasadena. After that she'd made a living as a waitress, working various bars, including a brief stint at the Rose City Lounge in the early 1960s. It had a Tahitian decor even then, and Roland could remember the morning she brought home the tiny carved-jade tiki idol, stringing it on a gold chain for good luck. "They give that to you?" he had asked; he was probably ten then, skinny and allergic to milk. "They didn't give me anything. I stole it." In those days the waitresses at the Rose City wore floral sarong skirts with matching halter tops, and Roland's mother complained every morning, as she pushed eggs around a pan, about having to show her belly button on the job. She quit the Rose City after an incident with one of the other waitresses, a girl who packed an abalone-handled knife in her purse. Roland never found out what happened. When he asked his mother, she said, "The last thing I'm going to do is stand around and be accused."

It was years ago, all of this, though it could have been yesterday.

Or today.

———

"Have you been practicing?" Michael asked at the driving range.

"Only a little." Every now and then he'd hit out a bucket on his own, when it struck him that he had nothing to do and Holly was too busy to give him a chat and his favorite soaps were interrupted with breaking news; he owned a club, an old-fashioned woody, bought at a yard sale for a dollar, and with it under his arm he'd head down to the range not to practice his swing but to inspect the traffic: You never know where he'll cock his head.

"Is everything okay?" Michael asked. "You look a little pale. You haven't been sick, have you, Roland?" There'd been a scare at the doctor's this week over a strange purple blotch on his wrist—you know the kind—but it turned out to be nothing more than an age spot. Not that an age spot is an easy thing to accept. But then Michael was backing away from his comment, stumbling a bit with: "I mean of course you're looking as good as ever, just a little paler is all. If only we all could hold up as well as you. I'm always asking myself: How does Roland keep away the years?"

Roland teed up the first ball. They'd started printing ROSE CITY on the balls last month to keep people from pocketing them. "Who'd want to steal these beat-up old balls anyway?" asked Michael. Roland didn't answer; just as he didn't answer how he kept away the years. You don't tell your secrets, Michael! The complex and ever-adjusting combination of water-based diet, exfoliating cream, and lying that went into the effort of keeping away the years would startle Michael if he were to learn the truth. So typical, to think Roland would tell him the truth.

Roland swung, and the ball sailed toward the net at the end of the range. "That's a great shot, Roland. Go on, hit another."

Roland fished a second ball out of the bucket and set it in place on the rubber tee. No other golfers next to Roland and Michael, but there were others at the range, mostly men in shorts revealing shins gone hairless, and Roland could hear the *swish* of drivers and steel-head woods, and the small knotted *pop!* of the balls lifting from their tees. In the booth where they sold the buckets a radio was playing, a pop song Roland didn't recognize. *Young and old, hot or cold, I'll still love you, you, you.*

"Do you mind if I give you a pointer?" asked Michael.

"Not at all."

"Pay more attention to your stance. Spread your feet some more, open the thighs. Yes, like that." His hands fell on Roland, guiding his legs apart and angling the bend in his knee. For such a large man, they were surprisingly gentle hands. Roland wouldn't have guessed that about Michael; you'd expect his hands to rip you in two. Just as Roland would never have guessed that Graham's hands, long and bony with a faint purple beneath the nail, were wired with a will of iron, taking Roland's wrist that first night at the Miyako Inn and not letting go. It had been Roland's idea to live together. He told Graham that the two of them should tell the world to go fuck itself. "Why would we want to do that?" Roland found an apartment off El Molino, in a complex called the Date Palm Court. Vietnam was still a thing to keep an eye on then, and during their first fight Roland got Graham so angry over the smallest of infidelities—*I didn't even know his name!*—that Graham's furious fist caused a candle to touch the cloth on the table, erupting it into flames. They extinguished the fire right away, but afterward Roland began calling the apartment complex the Napalm Court. "Are you taking me back to the Napalm Court? Are you trying to burn me up alive again? Is that what you want?" Roland would yell whenever they had an argument in a restaurant or, worse, in Mrs. Paires's living room, and all Graham could do was pick up Roland, legs kicking, and drive him home, easing him into bed with a blue sleeping pill.

Roland said to Michael, "How about ordering us some drinks?"

"What can I get you?"

Roland told him the usual, disappointed that Michael had yet to learn his order. Michael rushed off to the bar window, returning with an iced tea and a Manhattan in a red plastic cup, two cherries bobbing at the rim. Roland felt like saying *Thanks, Doll,* but instead pressed together a smile. "Now it's your turn. Go ahead and have a swing."

"No, no. Hit some more. I enjoy watching you."

"Oh, Michael," Roland said. "You're too much." Another ball on the tee, another swing, another whoosh, and there it went, up over the Bermuda grass littered with hundreds of balls, up up and up, but then—you're not going to believe this—Roland's ball hit another midair. If it weren't for the pop song on the radio, *Hot or cold, young and old,* Roland was sure he would have heard the crack of the two balls colliding.

"Did you see that?"

"See what?"

"My ball? Did you see my ball?" But Michael was making a face that tends to befall large men who are smart but not all that smart: lips turned up in the corner, eyes wide and moist, chin tilted toward the sun; he hadn't seen the balls collide. Michael hadn't seen anything at all.

So whose ball was that? Whose ball had dinged Roland's in midair? He scanned the line of golfers: Fifteen or twenty feet away was a man he hadn't noticed before. The man was nearly as tall as Michael, though not as hunky in the middle, with dark hair cut close, a goatee, and a gold hoop in his ear, maybe ten years younger than Roland; maybe twenty. The man waved. "Sorry about that, pal."

"I've never had anything like that happen to me before."

"Me neither, pal."

"It's uncanny."

"Sure is, pal." The man was wearing shorts high on his waist and a flowered shirt, a couple of buttons opened at the throat. He gave Roland the peace sign; he had to think back to the days at the Napalm Court to recall the last time someone had flicked Roland the peace sign.

"What's uncanny?" asked Michael.

"Oh, never mind." And then, turning again to the man, "Say, I haven't seen you here before. What's your name?"

"Name's Johnny. I'm here from time to time." He dug in his golf bag for an iron.

"I'm Roland. And this here's Michael."

Johnny nodded and then teed up. He was a lefty, which meant he faced Roland as he swung: The next ball shot like a bullet across the range.

"When we're done we can go into the lounge for a bite if you'd like," said Michael.

"Oh, all right, but only the salad bar for me. I love their diet Thousand—" He stopped, but didn't know why. Again he was struck with that feeling: something this morning he had forgotten to do. No appointments, no bills due in the middle of the month. He hadn't forgotten to show up at work because he didn't have work to show up to: His veteran's disability got him through the days. Not a week in Saigon and he'd been stabbed in a park around the corner from the Rex Hotel, beneath a coconut palm green in the trunk. Shouldn't have been in the park in the middle of the night, but he was. Shouldn't have been lurking in the hibiscus bush, but he was. His disability plus the little he skimmed from his mother's checking account got him through the days. His mother, living the way she did in the home down in Carlsbad, had more than enough. You see, his mother, after all those years, had watched her luck change; one night she showed up for work at the Mission, a bar out on Colorado, and guess who walked in? He did! Who, you're asking again? Who walked in? Her hubby-hub, her very own, a retired schoolteacher with a cedar-shingle bungalow in Altadena and a pension fund to carry her through the years after he was gone.

"I saw your commercial again," Roland said. "It was on after my favorite soap."

"Which one was it?"

But this caught Roland in a little white lie because he hadn't seen the ad, he'd said so only to make conversation, to make Michael feel good. Roland bent down to tee up another ball for Michael. He would ignore the question. Yes, that would be best.

Michael swung and said, "You look good with a little less sun. It suits you, Roland."

"I've been too busy for sunbathing. And besides, the lawyer's planning a dinner dance out by the pool tonight. The yard's been taken over by a big white tent. They're celebrating their twentieth anniversary, the lawyer and Holly. Twenty years, if you can imagine." Roland's doctor, the one who identified the age spot, had warned him against sunbathing. The doctor had also said, "I hope you're being careful, Roland. Hope you're watching out for yourself."

If Roland ever got blue about his past, he would remind himself that it was the 1970s when he and Graham had lived together; you couldn't get caught cheating back then because cheating didn't exist. Sleeping around was no more promiscuous than going out to lunch and dinner on the same day. "But I thought everybody felt that way," he had said, in his defense. There were the times down at Venice Beach that Graham never knew about because Roland would return to their apartment smelling too much of sea salt and coconut oil for the odor of another man, possibly two, to seep through his pores. No, that wasn't how Graham had figured it out. It was at a Christmas party in the Hollywood Hills at Patrick and David's, when Roland left with an actor named Blalock who wore his hair feathered over his ears. How could Graham not add up the pieces, what with Roland sneaking into their bedroom at the Napalm Court on Christmas Eve, the bed ablaze in a blue glow from the twinkle lights wrapped around the balcony rail. Graham had asked him to make a promise, one Roland knew he'd end up breaking even as he uttered the words. And so Graham threw Roland out, on a Friday afternoon, in the middle of his favorite soap.

"Oh boy, was Graham's mother a tough one," Roland said to Michael. "She'd give us a look, with her pointy little chin. She hated me. Blamed everything on me."

"She changed, Roland."

"People don't change. Oh, that chin."

"The world's changed, Roland."

"You don't have to tell me."

"She came to love me like a son," said Michael. Mrs. Paires had died a couple of years back, ashes hurled across Pasadena from the lookout on Mount Wilson; probably the only illegal thing Graham did in his life, scattering his mother like a litter-bug. Then, not long after, his own ashes followed, released from a balsa-wood box by the mild hands of Michael.

Roland studied Michael, his full pout. We've all got to move on, Roland was thinking, chewing his cherry. Last week there'd been a woman at the bar inside who could tie a cherry's stem into a knot with her tongue. The woman said she and Ted Kennedy's wife shared that particular talent. Not his wife the drunk, but his current wife, whoever she was.

"What about you, Roland?" asked Michael. "Do you ever see yourself settling down?"

"Me? Settling down? Of course I see myself settling down, Michael. Every single day." He was an odd one, this Michael, which figures why Graham took to him. He wore sunglasses on a cord around his neck and a uniform of pleat-front khakis, and Roland had seen him in nothing but white sneaks. And rich, as it turned out: not only a marketing exec but investments in a couple of gas stations and a car wash called the Mighty Clean.

"Did Graham ever tell you about all those times he came home from the office and found me with bags and bags of clothes from JCPenney? The whole living room covered with Penney's bags, and he'd always tell me to take everything back, every last thing. But I'd tell him he'd have to take it back himself and he'd say he would but he never did. So typical of him. Did Graham ever tell you about that?"

"No."

"He got so angry I was sure he'd talk about it the rest of his life."

"He never mentioned it."

"Well, I'm sure it was Graham," but then Roland realized it hadn't been Graham at all.

"Graham never uttered a bad thing about you, Roland."

And Roland stood back, the sun forcing a squint; what would make Michael say something like that?

And then, what had Roland forgotten to do?

Michael pulled a six iron from his bag and hit a ball. "Form is everything," Michael would say, and he had textbook form—knees bent, elbows bent, eye on the ball—though somehow his power could overwhelm it: The ball lifted and cracked to the end of the range, landing yards beyond the other balls, like an eager dandelion.

"How's the swing today, Johnny?" Roland called, waving him down.

"Just fine."

Michael looked over his shoulder at Johnny, his face grumpy in that way that told you Michael was on the verge of becoming an old man.

"We're just out hitting a bucket or two. Soon enough we're going inside for lunch."

"That'll be nice, pal," and Johnny bent his knees, moved his hips back, elbows up, and: Fore!

"Did you see that shot, Michael?"

"Missed it."

"Now, that's a shot." And this time through the megaphone of his hands: "Now, that's a shot, Johnny!"

"Do you know that guy?" Michael asked.

"Who, Johnny? Never met him in my life."

Michael moved to hit another ball while Roland took a load off on the bench. It was a hot day, and Roland sensed that he was bubbling up at the hairline and above his lip. And the chain around his throat, anchored by the little jade tiki idol, felt clammy with perspiration: And that was it! That's what he'd forgotten to do, stop by the Zale's in the Pasadena Plaza and get the chain's clasp fixed. It'd been popping open lately; he had nearly lost the pendant down the drain of the shower at the club.

He'd stop by after lunch. And while he was there give the old mall a cruise. You never know.

"What'd you say?" asked Michael.

"I didn't say anything."

"I thought I heard you say something about the Pasadena Plaza."

Roland shook his head and patted dry his forehead with a cocktail napkin, thinking of his mother. He should get down to Carlsbad one of these days for a visit. Hadn't dropped in since Mother's Day, when he showed up with the begonia in the foil. Not an easy trip for Roland, stopping in on his mother. He didn't like to think how old she was now, past eighty-five, there was no denying that. But things weren't all that bad for her: yellow curls still sitting up top, all the teeth there, eyes as blue as when she toted Roland around on her hip. A bit feeble in the legs, but holding up all right. Still turning some heads down at the home; or at least that's what one of the nurses, a 'mo with a diamond ring, told Roland last May. "All the widowers are after your mother," Nurse Kevin had reported. "They always were," said Roland, shaking out his shoulders and lifting his chin, as if the compliment were somehow meant for him. "And what about you?" Kevin had said next, giving old Roland a scan.

"Need another iced tea?" asked Roland.

"I'm fine now."

"Me, I'm going for a refill." He went to the bar window. A girl named Carol, barely old enough to drink herself, fixed him a second Manhattan. "Was it you I was telling about Ted Kennedy's wife?" From the window he watched Michael hit the ball. Farther down was Johnny, his shorts shifting as he swung, sweat pasting his shirt to his back. What was Johnny so focused on down there, never taking his eye off the ball, swing after swing? Roland thought about the woman who could tie a cherry stem with her tongue; how far could a talent like that take you? But look at Ted Kennedy's wife, whoever she was. Probably the only reason he married her.

When Roland returned, he found Michael looking at him in

that way of his: those full lips ajar as if he were thinking of something to say. Roland had to admit Michael wasn't so easy to figure out, his eyes gray with an impenetrability. Roland wondered why he could never read anything in those eyes; nothing to read, Roland had first assumed, but that had turned out not to be the case.

"Get the drink okay?"

"Of course, Michael. I'm a big boy."

"You know what I mean," he said, jamming his toe into the lawn. Graham had been dead only four weeks when they met at the ARCO station; more than once Roland had had to lend Michael a hanky to dab at the corner of his eye. Roland vaguely knew that Michael saw some part of Graham in him; knew that Michael was the type to live in the past. Roland didn't like that in a man. He was a forward-looker, saw the future as where his life would really begin. But they got along, chatting during their golf outings, and there were even a few afternoons when both had found themselves with nothing much to say. And Roland hadn't minded that, though he typically loathed a man who found himself at a loss for words. He took comfort in the heft of Michael at his side. He didn't think of him as his friend, though they were friendly; if he were to refer to Michael in conversation he'd call him his ex's ex. Once or twice Roland had said to Holly, "The good thing about Michael is he's so big that you can't help but notice him, so he's handy for snagging a wandering eye and then bringing it my way."

Roland flinched at the sudden touch of Michael's fingers on his neck. "Roland? Roland?"

And then, "Are you still thinking of taking that history course over at the city college, Roland? What was it you were thinking of taking, the History of Pasadena?"

"I'll take it one of these days. Maybe next semester. But I'm waiting for the right teacher. You know, there aren't so many people who know more about this town than me. I'm not going to take a class from any old someone. Almost anyone would be intimidated by having someone like me sitting at the back of the room."

"You're probably right about that, Rol."

"I can tell you the name of every Rose Queen for the last fifteen years. I can tell you when they had the first black Rose Queen. The first Asian Rose Queen. Remember her? Looked like Connie Chung, hair winged out like that. Filipino girl with a tough name to spell. The Rose Princesses wore maroon chiffon that year. Remember that year? Those toga dresses of maroon chiffon? I can tell you what the Rose Queen and her court wore for the last twenty-five years. Remember the year they put them in blazers and ties? They looked like a bunch of lady CEOs. That wasn't any fun, was it, Michael?"

"You sure have a memory, don't you, Roland?"

Roland made a noise like a pigeon.

"Remember that first day we met?" said Michael. "Remember how you told me all those stories about you and Graham, and I said you were like an elephant and you thought I meant you were fat?"

No, Roland didn't remember that.

"That'll be great for you," said Michael.

"What will?"

"Your class. Signing up for the class next semester."

"I'll do it if I can. I mean, things might be getting kind of busy for me soon."

Roland had taught Michael never to inquire further about such an open-ended comment. Better to leave his words hanging in the air than to turn to specifics, which on occasion proved missing. But Roland had no trouble looking ahead, knowing one day would be his day again. Not so far in the future he'd have a day of his own, that much Roland could count on. He was ready, too. That's why he aerobicized and beat back the bush and roasted his body brown as a ham. He was waiting for the heavy-knuckled rap. One day his hubby-hub would arrive at the apartment door and bang away until Roland opened up.

"Hey, Johnny. Sweet Carol made my drink so tall there's no way I can make my way through it alone. Can I offer you a sip?" He walked toward him, the plastic cup extended. Up close, Johnny was both less and more: biceps tight in the sleeve, a honk of a nose, two buttons open to reveal a waxed chest. It's what the faggy-fags were doing these days, waxing their chests and who knows what else. Not that Roland couldn't stand in a bar and hold his own; not that a good old-fashioned plucking didn't do the trick for him. Not so long ago, a young man with a face like a TV star had asked Roland to join him in the steam at the club. Not so long ago, someone told Roland that he'd like to pay him for the pleasure of taking him home.

"Not even a teeny-weeny sip?" Roland was saying to Johnny. He placed the jade charm between his lips and puckered up, an old standby that always caused a rise. I've still got it, thought Roland, returning to Michael.

"Some interesting things going on at the company," Michael said.

"Oh, yeah? Like what?"

"The newest things are mixed-race dolls. We've had to hire an agency to find people to model." Michael stepped back, relinquishing the tee to Roland.

"Exciting."

He took a swing but his club came down heavy on the base of the rubber tee, spilling over the ball. He bent to reset it, but as he rose a hyena-like burst of laughter interrupted his concentration.

One tee over, two men and a woman were dropping their golf bags, sliding sunglasses over their eyes, poking their mouths with the straws of iced coffees. Faggy-fags, Roland could see, eyeing the haircuts of the men: trimmed napes, hair gelled up spiky in front. A couple, you could tell. A couple and their gal-pal, out for a bucket of balls and a laugh. Roland had never seen so much traffic at the driving range, and he was about to point it out to Michael, but Michael cut him off: "Go on, Rol. Have another whack at it."

Roland took the driver.

"Watch your stance."

"Stay behind the ball."

"Think about your downswing."

Roland bent his knees and looked over his shoulder. One of the guys, a blond with boyish eyes and not much need to shave, was testing out a club, telling the others to stand back. But from the way the blond kept himself up, with his shirt pressed and starched and his mud-mask complexion, Roland knew what was going on. Roland could smell a betrayal on the wind. The other guy was balding, a creep of hair running from his back through the collar of his shirt. A few years older, a few pounds softer. From a distance you could hardly perceive the difference between the two men. But beauty's in the details; and Roland knew what was what. Why, just now the blond's eye was roaming up the row of tees to find Johnny Boy! Why, just now the blond was casting for eye contact with his man Johnny! The couple would last another two months, Roland surmised. Someone would tackle the other in a fit of jealousy; someone would abandon the other, screaming in the parking lot of Trader Joe's.

"We're testing out all sorts of ethnic combinations. Black-Chinese, Hispanic-Jewish, Asian–Native American," Michael was saying. "There are kids out there who come from couples like that, and they want a doll that looks like themselves. But you've got to get the colors right. The last thing a doll company can afford is a controversy."

"A what?" said Roland.

"A controversy."

"Oh, yes. By all means, avoid that, Michael."

Hard to know which way to look, with Johnny on one side and the blond on the other. Hard to know who to smile at and twist the necklace around his finger. It was something his mother had taught him. Not that she sat him down and gave him a lesson in flirting with a flimsy gold chain and a tiny idol of jade; no, instead he would watch her ready herself for a night out of waitressing and whatnot: the folding card table in the corner of her bedroom used as a beauty stand; the plastic hand mirror, the glass jar holding no-shine pads; the way he'd sit on the bed and she'd talk to him, not looking at him, applying the Jungle Red lipstick and the foundation. "Pay attention to your foundation," she used to say, not really to Roland. But he took note. The dab of gardenia oil in the fold of her elbow; the powder across her breasts; the foil-wrapped mint tucked into her bra. "Just in case!" And if Roland had written it in a notebook he couldn't have remembered the details any more clearly. Those evenings more familiar to him than most of his own. Standing at the mirror in the locker room, tweezer jammed up his nose, who do you suppose he was thinking of, who do you think was propelling Roland along? She was living proof, Roland kept telling himself. His mother was living proof: Live long enough, and everyone's hubby-hub shows up at the apartment door. The trick was to keep yourself from barking: "What took you so long?"

And now Michael was going on about something to do with the shopping mall. "Did you hear about the Pasadena Plaza?"

"Someone else murdered at JCPenney?"

"No, Roland, but you'll never believe it."

But Johnny was teeing up the final ball in his bucket; he'd be gone in a matter of moments. His club hit the ball so hard Roland couldn't follow its arc. Then Johnny began tidying up: clubs in the bag, towel mopping his brow, shirttail returned to the waist of his shorts. A second shriek of laughter from the threesome, this time louder and deeper, as if something filthy had been said. The blond was turning red in the throat; his boyfriend's mouth hung open, glossy with a bit of drool. The gal-pal, pretty, red hair, too thin, freckled, a trace of green in her skin, stepped up to the tee, swinging with better form than both the guys. Typical. Then Roland caught the blond sending a wink over to Johnny. Make that six weeks. These boys wouldn't last another six weeks.

"Isn't that incredible, Rol? That they'd do that? That progress turned out not to be progress at all?"

What was Michael talking about now? Of course he was a trannie, down from Bakersfield. Son of an oil-field worker, heir of nothing. "I was on my own. No one ever helped me along," he once told Roland. "No one until Graham." They bought the house on Lombardy, not the biggest on the block, but they fixed it up and grew a wall of bamboo around the backyard. After a few years, they dug a pool. Their neighbors were all in the Junior League, but no one seemed to mind the two of them, Michael had reported at one of their first outings. "No trouble in all those years. They were always as nice as can be, treating us just the same," he said. *Just the same:* That's what he thinks! Poor old Michael. Not a Junior Leaguer in the world who could deliver a banana bread to the new faggy-fag neighbors without thinking at least once of attaching a card that read: Please leave.

"Johnny," Roland called out. "I'm having trouble with my form. Do you think you could stop by and give me a quick demo?"

But Johnny was busy packing his golf bag, and he held up his finger, asking Roland to wait.

"I'm repapering the guest room," Michael said. "Well, not me. I've got a good paperhanger. A real nice guy." Michael took a load off as well, plopping on the bench beside Roland. "Plaid," he said. "A nice plaid paper."

"Oh, yes," Roland said. "Plaid. Sounds like you." Now Johnny flipped open his cell phone and was making a call. Roland wanted to yell, "Johnny, would you hurry up?" But he restrained himself. What was it his mother used to say? "As long as he wants you more than you want him, you'll be fine."

The two men and the redhead were discussing a movie, and Roland tried to hear which one. It had the word *love* in the title, that's all he could make out. But Roland couldn't think of a movie he'd seen recently with *love* in its title.

"Paper's a tough thing to pick out," Michael continued. "Maybe plaid isn't right. Maybe you could give me a hand, Roland. Graham always said you had a good eye."

That's what Mrs. Paires had said about him as well. Roland and she went shopping once for lamps, and when he found one with a glass-jar base, she'd said, "Such a good eye." It was the single nice thing she said about him. Roland used to wonder if she knew he cheated on her son, but that was impossible. People like Mrs. Paires, who was as Junior League as they come, didn't think like that. She didn't have it in her. And what about Michael? Had Michael ever heard the stories? Was he the type of man to assume the sleaziest? Even after a year, Roland couldn't be sure. But surely Graham must have told him why he threw Roland out.

But let's not visit old times. No point in that; it can be as disturbing as stepping on Scotty the Scale.

"It's a nice house, Roland," Michael was saying. "Bigger than it looks from the outside. A sunroom, too. And now with the bamboo, the back is real private. Graham and I used to sunbathe in the nude."

"Sunbathe in the nude?" Roland could hardly believe Michael had said that. "Who, Graham?" Wasn't Graham the one who refused to swim at the old Pasadena Athletic Club during the naked hours? Wasn't he the one with the shoulders that would sizzle even on a cloudy day, with the swim trunks hanging shyly to his knees? There are some things you don't want to hear about your dead ex, and that was one of them, he told Michael.

But speaking of sunbathing in the nude: Once Roland took his mother to Hawaii. Right before he checked her into the home in Carlsbad. A package deal to the Maui Prince Hotel, with its lobby aviary and sunset hula show and free vanda orchid on the breakfast tray; round the bend was a nude beach where Roland met a man who turned out to be an avocado farmer. Got such a bad sunburn that Roland had to spread a jar of Noxzema across his ass that night. "You ever been to Hawaii?" Roland asked Michael.

"Sure," he said. "Graham and I used to love Hana. You know, the road to Hana."

"We can get married over there," Roland said.

Michael stood from the bench, pushing the titanium driver toward Roland. His face flickered and lit up, a tremble in the lip, a flare in the nostril. "Roland? What do you mean?"

"We can go over there and get married. It's incredible."

"What are you talking about?"

"The new laws. There are new laws in Hawaii that let us get married."

"In Hawaii? Are you sure?" Michael said. "I thought it was Vermont. Isn't it Vermont where we can—"

Roland hoped to return to Maui one day, to the nude beach

round the bend. If he could ever scrape the money together, he'd jet over for a week. What with these new laws, there's bound to be a hubby-hub or two on the beach. Just last month he asked his mother for the money, but she said she couldn't spare it, her voice swallowing itself on the phone line. "Fixed income and all." As if she had to tell Roland.

Then Johnny appeared at their side. "Okay, I've only got a sec, I'm meeting someone inside for lunch."

"Don't miss the diet Thousand Island. It's to die for, Johnny."

Michael seemed to take a step away. Roland thought about introducing them, but then what was the point? This moment would come and go before Roland knew it; why waste time with Michael? Then Johnny's phone rang again and he moved away from them in the direction of the blond, taking the call, a finger in his ear.

"You thinking of going back?" Roland asked. "To Hana?"

"Hadn't thought about it." Michael's eyes lifted. "No one to go with, I suppose. Unless . . ." but Michael failed to finish.

The couple and the redhead decided they would call it a day as well, but they hadn't even finished a quarter of their bucket. Why were they leaving so soon? What about all those balls? "I'm starving," the boyfriend said. The girl said, "Let's go inside for a grilled cheese." They moved to collect their things, and the blond put his hand on the other man's shoulder, leaning in to whisper. Six weeks, Roland thought again. Give them six weeks. When the three were gone, they were replaced by a pair of businessmen, rep ties curving around their guts, fingers growing fat over ten-karat wedding bands. But before the businessmen began hitting out balls, they realized they needed a drink, and one of them volunteered to pay Carol a visit. He moved to the window, bumping into Johnny on the way.

"Maybe we could go someday, Rol?"

He wasn't sure when Michael had started calling him Rol, and it made him nervous, reminding him of something but he wasn't sure what. Then again came the nagging feeling: He'd better not forget to stop by Zale's. "What's that, Michael?"

"Maybe we could go someday."

"Where's that?"

"To Hawaii."

Johnny folded away the phone; if he'd been a few feet closer, Roland could have spied his number on the display.

"Rol?" And then again, "Rol?"

"What'd you say?"

"Maybe we could go to Hawaii sometime."

"God, sorry," said Roland. "Go to Hawaii? To hunt for a hubby-hub? With *you*?"

There'd been others since Graham, since Linda. A gemologist in San Diego, who first told Roland about the home in Carlsbad. A lab technician in Ojai, but he was too attached to his collie to squeeze Roland into his bed. A German banker who liked to bite Roland's thigh. An actor from New Jersey who never acted in a thing. A diabetic young man with a bump on his nose, his head crammed with political ambition. A VCR repairman who asked Roland if he was for real. A screenwriter tapping away at the computer in the night. A caretaker, bearded and holed up in a garage apartment like Roland's. A lawyer burdened by an affair in the past with his own brother. A bellhop living on a boat in Marina del Rey. A judge's son, with a mop of blond hair Roland would always miss. A medical student from Reno, the only person with a tan line darker than Roland's. An accountant who abandoned Roland one night at the Salt Shaker, bill unpaid. A rare-book collector who asked Roland to slip on linen gloves before handling his books, and his cock. A man named George, a mail sorter at the Burbank airport. An heir to an orange fortune who told Roland he'd love to take him home one day to meet his father, *wouldn't that be a laugh?* A business student who later turned up in the *Star-News* for shooting a dog. A guy out buying an anniversary gift for his wife. A risk manager, whatever that was, bragging about giving his last boyfriend a Porsche, but Roland ended up with nothing at all. A plumber with a baby girl named Star. A shop clerk with a reliable lock on his stockroom door. A delivery man from Bristol Farms in a bloodstained butcher's apron. A drama coach, a computer manual writer, a gardener with green rubber boots, a priest, make that two priests, Father Ricky and Father Jim, a wallpaper hanger—he was a nice guy. Hundreds of others, to tell the truth, but he had lived only with Graham. All the others lasted a few months, a few weeks, a few days. Each ended with a fib, an infidelity, a secretly borrowed credit card. But it wasn't always Roland's fault. Sometimes they'd up and leave Roland, no reason at all. If only he could marry, Roland thought often, boiling it down to this. It was because he couldn't marry that he'd blown so many chances. Marriage would force him to change his ways. Would give him more of a stake in the world. Would let him say to the man winking at the door to the steam, "I can't. I've got to get home—"

His hubby-hub was waiting.

"Getting hungry?" Michael asked.

"Can't wait to hit the salad bar."

"Now, what can I show you?" said Johnny. His shirt had split open another button, revealing more waxed chest. Maybe Roland should try a wax and a peel. What did he have to lose? That's what he was thinking, and: How could Michael not even take a peek at Johnny Boy? Was Michael even alive? His blood-less cheeks made you wonder. If Johnny didn't stir up old Michael, who could flip his switch?

"You been to Hawaii, Johnny?" Roland asked. "Been to Hana?"

"Just Waikiki; it was pretty. Climbed into Diamond Head and saw a snake. A green one."

"A snake!" Roland squealed. "Did you kill it?" He scooted closer to Johnny. "I bet you ripped it in two with your bare hands!"

Roland couldn't help himself; something would flutter up in his chest and carry him noisily to every man in the world. Yesterday there was the garbage man collecting the Dumpster from behind the lawyer's garage. A garbage man fetching Dumpsters! Even Roland had to admit there was no chance of him being his hubby-hub; the garbage man had clapped his industrial mitts and said, "You're pathetic, man."

"I didn't think there were snakes in Hawaii."

Was that Michael picking on Johnny Boy, calling him a liar? No snakes in Hawaii? You'd laugh if it wasn't so infuriating: Michael insisting on the truth even when it didn't matter. It made Roland shudder. Michael and that hair, thick as a young man's; really, the only thing they had in common was that each had held off the years better than most; that, and of course Graham. And then Roland remembered that Michael once told him that he used to call Graham his little cracker. What a name! And you know what, he couldn't help but think that maybe Graham had gone a little crackers during his years with Michael. Why else would he have stayed with him, this big dog of a man who claimed to know a thing or two about love? An image filled Roland's head: Michael and himself crossing the threshold of a suite at the Maui Prince Hotel, vanda-orchid leis around their throats, looking at each other uncertainly and pondering the future.

"We can get married there," Roland heard himself saying. "In Hawaii."

"Roland," snapped Michael. "What are you talking about?"

"Excuse me?" said Johnny.

"Those of us who are interested in settling down can fly over there for a quickie wedding. People tell me it's turning into *our* Vegas, or whatever."

"I'm not sure I know what you're talking about."

"Maybe that's because you're not the type to settle down, Johnny."

"Would you mind telling me what you're talking about?"

"Come on, Johnny, you know. Commitment ceremonies and all that. We can get married in Hawaii nowadays."

"Well, I suppose that's nice for you."

"What do you mean, nice for you?"

"I mean just that. What do you mean?"

Roland began to stutter, accusing Johnny of something, but Michael's hand fell to his side. "Roland."

"I'm kind of lost, pal. I thought you wanted a tip on your swing. I thought you wanted a pointer on your form."

"But I'm talking about getting married."

"Married?" said Johnny. "You're getting married? Listen, guys, I've got someone waiting for me in the lounge. I'll have to say so long."

"Yes, thanks," said Michael. And then, "Sorry about all this. A bit of confusion." Michael took Roland's wrists.

Johnny heaved the bag's strap over his shoulder and turned to leave, bumping into the blond.

"Sorry about that, pal," said Johnny.

"No trouble," said the blond, letting Bonnie Prince Johnny pass. And there he went, leaving Roland with that feeling he was all alone; the inevitability of it was beginning to exhaust him.

"*He*'ll know," said Roland, pointing.

"Excuse me?"

"I have a question for you."

"Yes?"

"No, make that two questions. First, what's your name?"

"Harry."

"Okay, Harry. We're having a little debate over here. Is Hawaii our Vegas, or isn't it?"

"What?"

"We were wondering," interrupted Michael. "We're sorry to bother you, but we have a question. Do you know anything about these gay marriage laws?"

"A little."

"Like what?"

"I know that in Vermont there's a new law where we can get some sort of civil union. Don't know anything more about it than that."

"Vermont?" said Roland.

"Yes, that's what I read, too," said Michael.

"I'm not exactly sure what it means, to tell the truth," said Harry.

"Vermont?" Roland repeated. "Are you sure it's Vermont?"

"Oh, it was definitely Vermont. It was in all the papers."

"I didn't read it in the *Star-News,*" said Roland.

"That's not a surprise. The *Star-News* is a bit conservative, isn't it?" said Harry. "There's a lot of things you're not going to read in the *Star-News.*"

"Are you sure it's not Hawaii? Who ever heard of eloping to Vermont? That doesn't make any sense. Doesn't it snow there? Doesn't the whole place freeze over in winter? It's probably covered in ice right now. Probably won't thaw out till spring. What am I supposed to do if I want to get married this week?"

"Are you two . . . you know," said Harry, "thinking about doing some sort of ceremony? Are you two together?"

But rather than let Roland answer that one, Michael replied, "Us? Oh, no, we're friends. We're not a couple. We're not . . ." He was blushing, his jaws churning, looking like he was going to say something else. Funny to see such a big man redden up and hit a loss for words.

"But it is sort of interesting, isn't it?" said Harry. "The possibility of getting married and all. Charles—that's my boyfriend who was here with me—we've talked about it. We're thinking about going through with some sort of ceremony."

"You *are?*" said Roland. "The two of *you?*"

"We haven't decided yet. It's a big decision. You know, marriage isn't all it's cracked up to be. It's not always love and happiness forever."

"Not for some people it isn't." This was Roland, who was sitting on the bench, propping his head on the shaft of his club. He wasn't feeling well, the sun catching up with him. He hadn't eaten all day; following a quartered-orange diet all week.

"Well, if you don't like Vermont there's always Denmark," Harry said. "Now, I know we can definitely get married over there. Wedding ceremonies, taking each other's names, the whole bit."

"Denmark!" cried Roland. "What am I supposed to do in Denmark? I'm not going to Denmark. First of all, I don't like blonds. I like them dark, like Johnny Boy. Wouldn't touch a blond with a ten-foot pole. You want me to go off to Denmark and marry a great big Dane? Is that what you're saying?"

"Listen, guy, I didn't mean anything by it." Harry began to back away, returning to the bench where he'd forgotten his sunglasses.

Michael shifted, touching his head. "Maybe we should go," he said. "Maybe we should skip the lunch and go."

Harry left them, crossing to the lounge. The businessmen had stopped hitting and were staring at Roland and Michael. What were they looking at? What was everyone looking at? Roland could blame it all on men like them, men sweating and panting from the swing of a golf club, men who kept him from settling down and marrying who he wanted. Roland felt the world close in on him: Would he really have to move to Vermont to marry the man of his dreams? Take up on a dairy farm at the foot of the Green Mountains in order to live the life he wanted? It didn't make sense. It left Roland wondering what he would have to do next.

Roland and Michael stood at their tee, silent. Carol showed up with a tray and a notepad. "Is everyone all set with drinks?"

"I think so," said Michael.

"Is Johnny inside?" said Roland. "Did Johnny go inside?"

"Roland, please. Forget it," said Michael.

"Who, Johnny? Yeah, he's in there, having lunch with his wife."

Michael packed up his clubs and prodded Roland toward the parking lot.

"Don't forget about our happy hour tomorrow night," said Carol. "Two-for-one in the lounge till ten. Free buffet. Buffalo wings, wontons, fried cheese. A real nice spread, Roland."

Roland's throat suddenly felt sore, as if he were still talking although his lips sat firmly upon one another. He teetered, and felt Michael behind him, propping him up. "Good-bye, Carol," said Michael.

Of course, technically Linda had been a blond. His hair was darker than Michael's, a lot darker than Graham's, but if you read his driver's license—which Rol did every night in high school after he'd swiped it from Linda's wallet—it said blond. There was a night in their senior year, at a post-prom party over on San Rafael, when Roland and Linda found themselves waiting for a bathroom to free up and then found themselves in there together, the door bolted, Rol on his knees. It happened only once, and Linda never spoke to Roland again, never on the football field, never again in Western Civ. The next time Roland tried to approach Linda, his fist yanked the chain from Roland's throat and hurled the jade pendant into his eye. Yes, that had ended it all between Roland and Linda, and off trudged Linda to Vietnam. Oh, what a day it was for Roland when he read it in the *Star-News:* LOCAL FOOTBALL STAR KILLED ON THE BANKS OF THE PERFUME.

In the parking lot the sun was harsh and blank. Roland put on his sunglasses and it made him think of a movie when the actress covered up a black eye with a pair of dark glasses at lunch. Except Roland didn't have a black eye; just felt that way.

"You've been coming to the Rose City at night?" Michael asked.

"Sometimes. For a drink or two. When I can't sleep. Or on my way home from the Miyako. You never know where he's waiting."

"Who?" And then, "I see."

They walked to Roland's car. In the parking lot near the patio, a truck was delivering party rentals: round tables and mint-colored cloths and a couple of kids in tank tops hauling collapsible white chairs through the side door. The sun beat down on Roland's neck, the smog sinking to the bottom of his lungs. There were mountains out there, the purple San Gabriels, dead dry chaparral and scrub pine leaning in their patient wait for rain, but you wouldn't know it today: the smoggy haze hanging like a fire curtain. For some reason Roland thought of the Napalm Court. He thought of the foothills going up in October flame.

"What were you saying about the wallpaper?" He thought about suggesting they see each other again, but decided to wait for Michael to bring it up, as he always did: pulling his Palm Pilot out of his pocket and proposing a date. "You were thinking of a stripe? I'm not so sure about a stripe. It depends on the size of the room."

"Thanks," Michael said. "I'll keep that in mind. But it's picked out already. It'll be fine." And then, "It's a nice plaid."

"Plaid?" Roland said. "Someone else was telling me about wallpapering in plaid." But Roland couldn't imagine who. "Say, I have to stop by the Pasadena Plaza, gotta run into Zale's for a second. Want to come along?"

"Roland, didn't you hear what I said?"

"Sure I did. What?"

"They're tearing it down."

"Tearing what down?"

"The Pasadena Plaza. It went bankrupt. The whole thing was a big mistake; the city decided they never should've built it in the first place."

A mistake? Wasn't it only yesterday that he and Graham had watched the old Athletic Club collapse upon itself to make room for the mall, the wrecking ball aloft like a great black sun? Not quite yesterday, but almost. Roland wondered if he could believe Michael, but why would he make it up? And if they could make a mistake on such a grand scale: Roland got a chill over all the other mistakes that must have infected his life by now. Such a bit of news didn't feel real, and he wondered why no one was talking about it. But maybe they were. It struck him as unfair. He didn't have to close his eyes to recall the smooth dark mass of the wrecking ball. Would they hire the same crane to tear down the mall? Would the little plaque memorializing the woman slain in the dressing room come down as well?

They were at Roland's Malibu, the towel wadded on the green vinyl seat. "You mean Zale's has closed, too?"

Michael nodded. "The whole place."

Oh Roland, Roland, striving for a place in the world: With whom does a man like Roland Dott belong? It was a question

Roland would never ask himself, but one the sagging corners of his eyes prompted others to ask for him. Roland waited for Michael's gentle hand, but it didn't come.

"Are you sure you can drive?"

"Sure I'm sure."

"You're going straight home, Roland? Just up the hill?"

" 'Course I'm going straight home. And what business is it of yours, anyhow?"

"I'm worried about you, Rol."

"Well, stop worrying about me."

"Roland. Give me your keys."

Michael touched him, but Roland pushed him away. Michael slipped and nearly fell but then he was righting himself. Roland couldn't think of what to say.

"All right then. Watch out for yourself, Roland. Be sure to take care of yourself."

"Sorry, what'd you say?"

"I said take care of yourself."

"I always do."

A few feet of pavement separated them, the diamondy bits of a broken bottle, and Roland didn't know if he should turn his cheek to welcome Michael's good-bye kiss or stand there and wait for the hug, and he felt a flicker catch in his chest as the sun pressed down on him; the sweat ran from his pores, beneath his arms, across the ribbed sweep of his back, inside his shaved thighs, all around his face, a halo of perspiration appearing at once to cast a glow across his brow and his chin, along the elegant ridge of his expensively shaped nose. And Roland's left hand, the one with the recently identified age spot, reached for the chain and the tiki idol; out of mindless habit his ring finger moved to coyly claw the necklace, to place the pendant between his lips. But the hand—bone and skin and freckle and tube of vein somehow bearing little of the wear and tear of Roland's past—found nothing clasped at his throat, nothing dangling against his much-admired chest. The necklace was gone, and with it, or so it felt, a panorama of memory loosened and tumbled away, leaving behind a dual look of shock and regret pinned to the face, still handsome after all these years, of our man Roland Dott.

TRESPASS

Through the hydrangea leaves Boyd and I watch San Rafael Road. We are hot and grimy, dirt rolling up in the fold of our elbows—my elbow, at least; Boyd won't show me his even if I ask. It's end of summer, sky smoggy brown, lawns yellow and prickly against the face, sprinklers *tick-tick-tick* spraying the dead grass. The hydrangea is limp in the branch, giving up, or at least that's how I look at it, the purple pom-poms withered and blown away so long ago that it seems now that they never could have existed, those fat blue flowers. We're bored, Boyd and me, bored with summer, with the heat, with the smog trapped in our lungs, bored with each other. Nothing to do, I've been complaining for weeks, and Boyd licks his chapped lips and says, "Don't blame me."

Earlier in the day Boyd asked me to join him in a round of Hubcap. We were hanging out in his driveway, and I hesitated. The old hydrangea bush, where Boyd and I once proclaimed eternal friendship, was beginning to feel like a hideout from someone else's childhood. Not so long ago I used to lie on the rotting leaves at the hydrangea's roots and wait patiently for Boyd. Used to rake up with my fingers the scattered pom-pom petals and make everything neat and nice for the two of us. Used to tell Boyd, "Meet me in the bushes," and feel something warm in my stomach.

"I don't feel like it today," I said when Boyd asked this afternoon. Not sure why.

Boyd, who'd been working on a skateboard scab all day, pried part of it free and flicked it in my direction. Then he asked again, and I said, as I always will, okay.

The hydrangea grows in a row along the far wall of Mr. Trader's mansion. Around Easter it bursts with flowery balls of lavender, pink, and white with a trace of blue. But every spring I used to sneak over to the bush and snip one or two blossoms and then run all the way home and offer them up—shyly, saying nothing, kind of hiding behind the bouquet—to my mom. But that was before Boyd told me how uncool I can be. "Sometimes I wonder about you, man."

Today there's the kind of heat when everyone bugs you, and

you're thinking *leave me alone,* and I'm thinking that as we crouch in the hydrangea, not so much about Boyd but about the whole world, and maybe what I'm really thinking is that I want the whole world to leave Boyd and me alone. I look at him and wonder if he's thinking the same, if he's ever thought the same. But Boyd's face—shaped like a valentine, with a dimpled chin and girly long lashes—reveals nothing: He's sitting next to his stack of stolen hubcaps, ready to shoot.

He's six months older, and you can tell if you know where to look: the dark hairs sprouting above his ankles, the thighs filling out his corduroy shorts, the lump behind his fly. He smells different now, too: dirtier. And his eyes, brown like mine—*Isn't it funny how we've got the same eyes,* I used to say before he snapped at me to cut it out—seem to have a hard time focusing on anything these days, especially me.

"My mom's taking me shopping for some new clothes tomorrow," I say.

"And you're telling me this because—?"

"Because I'm going to get some shorts like yours, with the Velcro pockets."

"Jesus, Mitch, what's up with you?"

I stop myself from saying, What do you mean? Maybe I don't want to know.

Almost an hour passes; traffic is light and none of the cars that slope down San Rafael match our collection of hubcaps. Boyd's getting antsy, I can see it in his twitching face, in the way he's rolling a tennis ball back and forth, and then he says, "This sucks. Hubcap's getting old." He gives me one of those looks that makes me feel like it's my fault. "Where are all the fucking cars?"

I try to think of something he might want to hear but I have no idea what that is, not anymore, and so I shrug my shoulders, and just then Boyd's ears prick up and he cocks his head. "Wait a minute. What's that?"

Up the road there's the sound of an engine coughing. Boyd begins to stroke a hubcap that came from a beat-up truck in the far corner of El Rancho's parking lot. "Sounds like a Chevy," he says. "It's definitely a pickup, a four-by-four for sure. You'll see." A few seconds later a silver Chevy with a lawn mower strapped into its bed careens past us. "Fuck," Boyd says. "We need to get ourselves a fucking Chevy cap."

The hubcaps are his, except for the spoked one that once belonged to the rear wheel of a Buick parked in a poorly lit section of the Pasadena Plaza's parking garage. I set out to steal it one day a few weeks ago when Boyd, pissed about nothing, said, "Fuck, Mitch. What good are you?"

The Chevy putters round the bend and we watch its belch of exhaust hang in the air; then it rises into the great blanket of smog. Boyd looks at his watch and says, "That's it for me, I'm out of here."

"Already?"

"I've got to go over to Mr. Bowman's."

"Who's that?"

"Some dude who lives around the corner from Jessica. The guy's on vacation and I'm taking in his mail and watering his plants and shit."

"Can I come?"

Boyd says no but I can tell he doesn't really mean it and so I begin helping him hide the hubcaps beneath branches. Then we hop out of the bush. "But you're not coming with me to Jessica's," he says, with a wink.

Boyd and I live in a neighborhood not far from Mr. Trader's mansion, though it might as well be another world. Where we live, the yards are small stamps of lawn, the ficus shrubs sheared into the shape of lightbulbs. Yellow stucco houses with white pebble roofs, aluminum gates leading to concrete patios. Mutts with matted fur chained to mailboxes, driveways stained with motor oil, Christmas lights perpetually strung along peeling eaves. A girl in a halter top watering a bed of pale dirt. A boy in a bathing suit splashing in an inflatable pool, hacking with asthma.

Jessica's richer than Boyd and me and lives in an area between Mr. Trader and us. Where she lives, the driveways are paved with brick and the houses rise up with cathedral-ceilinged entries and second stories, and nearly everyone on her block trains a bougainvillea up the side of their chimney. Two cars in each drive, SUVs with tinted windows, satellite dishes, redwood tubs of pink and white flowers guarding the front doors. Little signs planted in the lawn advertising an alarm system. When we pass Jessica's house, Boyd gives me a nudge with his elbow. "Did I mention her parents are out of town?"

I nod.

"Out of town for a whole fuck-me week."

Mr. Bowman, whoever he is, lives in a restored bungalow with a front porch, all of it hidden behind a redwood fence and a thicket of bamboo. "This way," says Boyd, opening a gate with camellia bushes standing tall on either side. "He likes me to use the kitchen door." Boyd holds up a key, and it flashes in the late afternoon, reminding me of something but I can't think what.

The blinds are drawn, and a cool gray veils Mr. Bowman's kitchen. There's a relief to it, the air soft as shade, the sunlight folded away. "Feels good in here," I say, but those words, and my cheerful tone, somehow sound—once I say them—inappropriate. "Who is this dude, anyway?"

"Some guy my mom met at the Pasadena Athletic Club. They take yoga together, if you can imagine." Boyd laughs, and I laugh, too, but I'm not sure why.

I follow him down a hall. On the walls are photos of a guy doing all sorts of sports: a man in a life vest on a white-water raft, the same guy in a helmet on the granite face of a mountain, two windsurfers, a man hoisting a snowboard above his head. "Is this Mr. Bowman? In all these pictures?"

"I don't know." And then, "Probably. All I know is he's a big ecotourist and crap like that. Bungee jumping over gorges, climbing in Alaska, that sort of stuff."

He unbolts the front door and fetches the mail from the porch. I'm waiting in the front hall, looking around, but there's nothing interesting to look at: On a side table a pottery lamp glazed in something that looks like milk. A glass bowl holding a ring of keys, a yellow diving watch, a photo of two men, nearly identical with red parkas and skis and goggles on their foreheads, their arms around each other. They're on a mountain next to a sign with a cap of snow that reads: *Attention! Vous vous trouvez sur une piste hasardeuse!*

"This guy gets a lot of mail," Boyd says. "All this today." He holds a bundle wrapped in a rubber band. "And a ton of magazines."

"What does he do?"

"Mom says he owns some Internet company. Something to do with sporting goods on-line."

"Damn," I say, and Boyd whistles too, because we don't know very many rich people except for the lawyers and doctors and men in blue suits and red ties who drive champagne-colored cars around Pasadena. We don't know any web millionaires, just old rich people like Mr. Trader, whose family made money in oranges.

This Mr. Bowman dude, there's something about him and his house that gets my mind running away from itself, on ahead into this part of my brain I think of as an open pasture where the grasses reach beyond my thighs and stalks of bluebonnets shiver in a breeze and the field is so vast that anything I want in it, and anyone, is there: my dog, Jane; a new BMW convertible; cupcakes with pink frosting and sprinkles; and some boys who I don't know but dream of anyway, waiting for me at the edge of a creek, waiting to pull off their shirts and shorts and skinny-dip in the dusk. And now in this pasture I see a man with a snow-board and ski goggles and a big smile and think maybe it's Mr. Bowman. Except I don't know who Mr. Bowman is and just as I'm about to start shooting the questions at Boyd—How old is this guy? Does he live here alone? Do you think that's his brother, the guy in the photo?—I realize I might give something away *(but what?)* by inquiring.

"Where'd he go on vacation?"

"Trekking in Nepal." In Mr. Bowman's living room Boyd sits on the couch, his legs yawning, giving me a peek of underwear. I don't want to look at that, the hint of white-brief mound up his thigh, and so I turn to Mr. Bowman's bookshelf and pretend

I'm looking at what he reads. But most of his books are travel guides, their spines cracked white. Next to me Boyd is sorting the mail into piles and he says, "My mom says I should keep his mail neat for him." He says it a bit defensively, as if he doesn't want me to think it's his idea to be thoughtful. He separates the mail into stacks of magazines, junk, bills, and envelopes that look personal and private. Boyd comes across a postcard and holds it up with a *what's this* look on his face and reads it. Then he tosses it to me. "Check it out."

On one side is a painting of a young man with a green ascot and a mop of sandy hair. The painting looks old, like a boy from a hundred years ago, and there is something in his pouty lips and pale cheek that makes me think of myself. The other side is smudged with a note:

You're right, three days in Barcelona isn't enough! Met a cute boy—black hair and eyes, skin like a fig's—named Arturo who took me to a tennis club and we played three sets on the finest clay I've ever seen. (Who cares that I lost!) Can't wait to hear your tales.

Lots of love, Jason

I drop the card, its tiny weight flipping over and over. Boyd and I watch it fall. Then from the rug the portrait of the messy-haired lad stares up at me, and a tremor rises in me in a single wave.

"The guy's a fag."

I try to look up from the postcard but can't. I can't look at Boyd. "How do you know?"

"Didn't you read the card?"

I read it again and then look to Boyd, as if he can explain something.

"The guy's a faggot, no doubt about it." He plucks the card from my hand and drops it in the pile of mail.

"Have you met him?"

" 'Course I've met him."

"What's he like?"

"What do you mean what's he like?"

"I mean, you know. Well, what's he like? What sort of dude is he?"

"What do you mean what sort of dude is he? He's a nice enough faggot dude with a lot of dough and a lot of boyfriends, as far as I can tell."

"How old is he?"

"How the fuck should I know? Maybe thirty." Boyd returns to sorting the mail, and I sit on the arm of the couch and try to imagine the man from all the pictures roaming the halls of the house, but my mind comes up with nothing but the image of him standing alone in my open pasture.

Boyd holds up a tissuey envelope and says, "Check out this one. Looks like a letter from his mom."

The letter is from Mrs. Eugene Bowman, Oshkosh, Wisconsin. "Do you think his mother knows?"

"Fags tell everybody these days. They think it's no big deal." And then, "Okay, I'm all done. Let's get out of here."

"What's no big deal?"

"That they're fags. Come on, let's blow this place."

"That's it? Don't you do anything else for him?" I keep looking at the envelope from his mother.

"I told you it's an easy job. I get twenty bucks for five minutes of work."

"What about watering his plants?"

"Only every other day."

"Even in this heat? It's a hundred degrees out there."

Boyd thinks about this. "Maybe you're right."

I follow him around the house as he noses a stainless-steel watering can into pots of spider plants and ivy and a struggling orchid. "You really think he's a fag?" I ask as Boyd trickles water into a yellowish fern hanging in the bathroom.

"Hey, it was my mom who told me first. Just look around this place, can't you tell?"

The bathroom reminds me of the one I share with my brother: square-inch tiles on the floor, bigger blue ones on the wall. A pile of towels on a rack, a couple of used ones curled in the corner. A stack of magazines next to the toilet, *Time* and *National Geographic* and *Sports Illustrated*, the same magazines my brother reads. The door to the medicine cabinet is open, and inside I scan for something to tell me more about the man who lives here: on the glass shelf the stem of a red toothbrush, a razor, a scum-rimmed glass, a bottle of blue cough syrup, a tube of hair gel, something called hyperrejuvenating hydrointensive exfoliating scrub.

"Look at those," says Boyd.

"What?"

"His stash of rubbers."

"Where?"

"Those round gold things."

"They look like chocolate coins."

"Don't try to eat one."

"Just because he's got some rubbers doesn't mean he's a homo."

"Trust me on this one, the guy's a 'mo. Now let's get out of here. Jessica's waiting." He drops a condom in his pocket and licks his lips.

Suddenly I feel slow and behind, incapable of catching up to the spin of the world. Boyd has said he's done it with Jessica, all the way, but has he really? There's no way to know. No way to know about so many things.

He switches off the light and returns to the kitchen. As I begin to follow, I look at the bathroom one last time. In the bathtub stall is a double-hung sash window with panes of bubble glass. A shred of sunlight pushes its way under the bottom of the window, and right away I know it is open and unlocked, that there is a way back into the house. With that bit of information ticking in my head, blowing through the pasture of my brain, I catch up with Boyd, tracing his steps across the kitchen and out the door into the cutting sun, the gag of smog, the cloy of Pasadena in the final sunburn days of August.

———

"Mitch, dear," my mother says, "How about another wing?" She floats a platter of barbecued chicken under my nose. I shake my head, and worry rises in my mother's eye. She's right to be concerned, because all I can think about is the crack of sunlight under Mr. Bowman's window. I can still see it floating in front of me, and it's as if that window—that window that needs a Windexing and a stronger latch—is my only way in and out of the open pasture. Sitting at the patio table with the smell of burned chicken skin rising in my nostrils, all I can think of, all I can see really, is that window. And with a shove, up it will go and through it I will climb. Is this making any sense? It doesn't to me, not just now, not with my mother, flat-chested in her sundress, saying, clucking, "Then at least eat your corn. Mitch? Dear?"

"I ate with Boyd."

Her head tilts; she doesn't believe me. Next to her my brother slumps, his teeth forging a row across the buttery cob of corn, and on her other side my father fetches a fallen shred of chicken skin from his lap and slurps it between his greasy lips.

"Boys," my mother announces. "Your father and I are going to the movies tonight. It's just too hot to stay home. Any takers?" My mother resembles a little girl, a tiny heart on a chain around her throat, hands small and pink, a ring with a dime-store fleck of diamond, her gold hair braided down her neck.

"No, thanks," says Charlie. "I'm going to Michele's. She's got A.C." He's seventeen, sideburns down his cheeks, stubble on his throat, already having trouble with nose hairs. Charlie plays running back on the football team, which might make you think that he's the dumb jock of the family and I'm the straight-A boy, and sometimes I believe it, too, but that's not the case. He gets better grades than I do and keeps his room tidier, and sometimes he stops by my room and sits cautiously on my bed and gives me a serious look and says things like, "You really need to start buckling down. Mom asked me to tell you so." Other than moments like that, which thank God are few and far between, he pretty much ignores me, ever since he found under my mattress—what was he looking for?—my stash of jockstraps stolen from the gym. The only thing he said about it was, with a gentle punch to the arm, "Can't figure out what size you are?"

"I was thinking of going over to Boyd's and then we might go to Jessica's for a swim."

"Sounds like the troops have plans," my father says. He's tall and pear-shaped: thinning hair; wide, dark eyes next to a fleshy nose. Most of the time I try to ignore how similar our faces are. "I want everyone home by eleven," he says. "The paper says they're starting the spraying then. Says they found another medfly on a lime tree in San Gabriel."

"I just don't understand how they find the little things one at a time," my mother says. "I mean, have you ever seen a picture of one? They're so *small*."

"Mitch, be sure to get back in time to bring Jane inside before they start spraying." The owner of a pet store, my father is particularly worried about the effects of the malathion on our Great Dane. "I mean it, Mitch."

"Mitch and I took an unscientific poll at the Price Club this morning," my mother says. "And we found that four out of five people don't believe the government on this malathion business. One out of two think they're overdoing it with the nightly spraying. And one third of all our respondents don't even believe the medfly exists. What do you think of that?"

"Proves the people know nothing about what's going to get them in life," my father says.

"Indeed."

When I was little I begged for a wall covered with corkboard in my bedroom, and now it hangs there, big and brown and ugly, and it's not coming down in my lifetime, my father says.

After dinner I've got nothing to do, so I lie on my bed and throw feather-tailed darts at the race-car posters. I'm thinking about one thing: the window, how easily it will lift, and the vast open space where I might find anyone, anyone at all. I wonder what Mr. Bowman's doing right now; probably middle of tomorrow in Nepal, and he's probably out on a trek with mud splattered on his calf, leading the way for one of his—do you suppose he really has one?—boyfriends. And the house sitting empty behind its wall of bamboo, and the window letting the smoggy wind creep in, and maybe something else. I wonder what would happen if I were to return to the house in the night and jimmy the window up and crawl through, finding myself standing in Mr. Bowman's house. What *could* happen? Of course I'd be breaking in, but not technically: Does it count as breaking in if you've already been in the house? I don't think so, but at the same time I know it must. But the window is open as if waiting for someone, and I could go there and no one would know where I am, and that is the best part of this dream and the beautiful picture of the window and the field in my head: standing in the dark house, the air cool, the world silent, alone in a new world, my new world, the world where I already know I belong.

Downstairs the front door slams. Charlie's off, over to Michele's; no doubt he's fucking her tonight, he'll sleep till ten in the morning, always does after visiting her. Comes down to breakfast with a smile and an appetite. Says things like, "Don't you have any bacon, Mom?" Fuck Charlie.

The front door closes again, latch not catching the first time but the second, then the scrape of the backyard gate opening and the stuttering first breath of my dad's car. I hold my own breath as they take their time. I can picture it: Dad fiddling with the mirror, Mom saying, Oh I forgot my purse, and Dad saying, Ah, honey, do you really need it, and Mom saying, No, I guess not. The car revs, as much as my dad will rev anything, and at last down the driveway they go, one final stop at the foot of the drive, probably because my mom turns to my dad and says, Do you think everything's all right with Mitch, and my dad replies, Honey, we're going to miss the movie. Then the engine fades into the night and things in my house fall quiet except for Jane's hungry howl.

Nothing else to wait for. Nothing at all.

It takes five minutes to reach the bungalow on my bike. I unlatch the gate and wheel in my bike, its chain clicking, *tisk! tisk! tisk!* Avocadoes cover the lawn, and one squishes beneath my shoe. There are no avocado trees in my pasture, only the bluebonnets and Queen Anne's lace and black-eyed Susans and the other wildflowers with their honey-semen scent, and so the avocado pisses me off because I picture the green track it's going to leave in Mr. Bowman's tub, down his hall. What if my avocado-smeared shoe somehow ends up on his bed, which I imagine is high off the ground and white and stacked with pillows half the size of me. The tree, with a skirt of ivy, blocks the bathroom window, but I wedge myself between it and the house. It feels as if I'm watching a movie and I'm the star, which doesn't sound so far-fetched because something in me thinks that someday I *will* be a star, and who doesn't think that?, but right now I'm sitting in the stadium-seating theater watching the flick and there's nothing I can do to stop the main character from going ahead and doing the dumbest thing he's ever done in his short and unremarkable life. If there were a soda to sip, I would. I am both frightened and enthralled.

I try shoving up the window screen but it's old, brittle and black with dust, and sharp like the invisible glass in those pink rolls of insulation. A few pricks to the fingertips aren't going to stop me, though, and I try some more. Nothing happens, and quicker than even I would have guessed I lose my patience and begin sawing the screen with my house key. At last the screen gives, and I cut two small slits so I can reach inside and find the latches. They are stiff yet there's nothing to do but keep working at them, and all sorts of things are going through my head: If Mr. Bowman is so rich, why doesn't he get new screens? And what if a neighbor hears the rustle in the ivy? And what do I possibly think I'll find in the house? But above all that is the loud call of someone shouting: *Go, go, go!* Like the voice of a coach standing at third base: Hustle on inside! Then my head silences and a small voice speaks up: It's never too late to go home. I recognize the frantic voice of shy Mitch Hatch chiming in, and already it seems to belong to another dimly remembered fourteen-year-old. Nothing is going to stop me: not even the boy I once was, who would have stayed home and gone to bed, smuggling a novel and a flashlight under the sheets. No, the boy I was before the first corn-silk hair sprouted between my legs is gone now, his final traces swept away, and as I raise the screen and then the window's lower sash, I whisper into the dark echoey space of Mr. Bowman's bathroom, "That wasn't really me, anyway."

The lamp in the front hall is on, and in its distant glow I can see what lies before me: a plain bathroom, which looks bigger from this angle. Standing in Mr. Bowman's tub, I touch his bottle of green dandruff shampoo, the same kind Charlie uses. I close the window and switch on the light. Gray scum glazes the bath, and a pad of dry hair lies like a lid over the tub's drain. This guy needs a maid. I go to the medicine cabinet—you'd think I have a plan from how fast I'm moving—and unwrap a condom. I roll the dusty latex in my hand and over my fingers and then put it in my pocket. The cabinet's other half holds more of the same: yellow mouthwash, a pack of Q-Tips, a cake of hand soap, a clear plastic bottle labeled "SLICK—The Personal Lubricant." Carefully I pick up the bottle, turning it like an artifact. Maybe this can tell me something about a fag's life. I squeeze a drop of the clear fluid into my palm and begin rubbing it into my skin like hand lotion. It feels like the perfumed oil Boyd's mom once brought back from a dude ranch in Arizona. One night last spring, when we began lifting dumbbells after school, Boyd invited me over and asked me to give him a massage with the contents of the little blue vial. "All great athletes get their muscles rubbed," he said as he lay on the maroon carpet in his bedroom. He was wearing baggy swim trunks, and as I gingerly worked the rose-scented oil into the skin of his arms and chest I watched a small lump rise in the nylon of his bathing suit. I told him I'd do his legs too, but instead he sat right up. "No way, only my arms are sore," he said, the corners of his mouth hanging down in distaste.

I return the bottle to the cabinet. My mind has gotten away from me, and without realizing it I've been rubbing the lubricant into my skin—my thighs and shins and stomach and neck—for nearly ten minutes, transfixed by the shellac it leaves. I clean myself with a washcloth, knowing that it's getting late, and all this thinking of Boyd—have I mentioned the way he likes to flex his muscles in front of the mirror?—has made me anxious. He's probably around the corner fingering Jessica right about now. She's probably getting ready to go down on him, licking her greedy lips. He's probably telling her he's taking in the mail for her homo neighbor, and they're sharing a nasty laugh as Boyd places his hands on her shoulders and pushes her on her way.

But there's still the mail to look at. In the living room I reread Jason's card. Only now, when I get to read it alone, do I understand what it's about. About one guy meeting another. Shit. It really can happen. I hold up the letter from Mrs. Bowman to a light. Is it possible that she knows? Is it possible that she doesn't care? Through the envelope I can make out the words "your father's fishing magazine." I flip it over. Against the lamp I can read something about "your news." And so, without thought, without reservation, with my head dizzy and my prick hard, my fingers crawl out of my pocket and slit the envelope's seam.

Dear Matthew,

I know it has been over a month since you wrote us with your news, but it still feels to me like it is the same afternoon that I opened your letter and that I am still standing in that awful hot sun we had in that heat wave in July. I started reading your letter in the driveway and the sun and your news just stopped me right there. (Dad and I have repaved since the last time you were here so you don't know how black and hot and tarry that asphalt is.)

Even though you thought it would not surprise us, well, it did. It really did surprise me is what I should say. It had never oc-

curred to me, never crossed my mind. I know, as you pointed out, that you never talked about dating girls in college or since you moved to California, but I always thought you just decided not to tell your father and me about them. Plus, you've always worked so hard I thought you were paying attention to your career just right now. We all know how competitive the Internet World is these days. Anyway, no, I never once thought of anything else, that you might be anybody else. Not just once. How could I?

So, I was standing there at the end of the driveway reading your letter, just all worked up by the news in the first paragraph, when Mrs. Broak, you know what a Mrs.-butt-my-way-into-everything she's always been, sneaked up behind me. She literally tiptoed right up behind me until she could look over my shoulder. Then, pretending to be casual, she asked, "What're you reading?" Well, she startled me so, and that sun and the wavy heat coming up from the asphalt and your news, everything just turned me around. Before I knew what I was doing I said, "Can you believe it? Everything in today's mail was junk, all garbage, nothing but missing children notices and book club offerings," and I lifted the lid to one of the cans at the end of the drive (it was trash day) and threw the whole day's mail into the garbage, bills, your father's fishing magazine, your letter, everything! She just startled me so.

When I finally got rid of Mrs. Broak, I went inside and sat myself down in the front window. Two houses down across the street I could see Mrs. Broak do the same thing in her living room window, and we both just perched, our eyes on the garbage can, me waiting for her to get up and go to the bathroom, she waiting for me to give in and go and dig the mail out of the trash. Now, I couldn't do that, not with the talk that would follow. So about 2 hours later I just watched the Garbage Men empty the trash cans into their truck and drive away the day's mail.

Not to worry, the bills of course came again the next month, and I went out and bought your father a new copy of The One That Got Away. *But your letter was gone and I never even finished reading it and of course I never got to show it to your father. Since then I have often thought that maybe I misread that first paragraph, and that it did not say what I thought it said. In fact I was nearly convinced of that until the other night when I was standing in the kitchen making a lasagna and all of a sudden I was struck that we hadn't heard from you in over a month. I said to myself, Joanie, things in life don't turn out as you planned for a reason, and maybe Matthew didn't marry Allie Shenk the way you were so certain he would when he was in the eighth grade, but you've only got one son on this planet, and that's one more than Linda Broak, so don't screw this up, Joanie, you hear me?*

Your father of course doesn't know anything about your letter but I think at some point we should tell him. So, what's the next step? Where do we go from here? Just like the time when you were in college when you took us on the foot tour of Boston (what was that called, the Freedom Trail?), that's a perfect example of how you've always been so good at showing us the way. We need you to do it again.

Love,

Mom

I look around Mr. Bowman's living room, a lump climbing my throat, and for the first time in my life I feel the regret of a committed crime. The envelope is slashed beyond repair. I fold the letter back into its envelope but somehow it ends up in my pocket.

Poor Mrs. Bowman. I imagine her waiting daily in her front-window chair for the mail to bring her son's response so they can reconcile. I picture Mr. Bowman coming home nightly in khaki trousers and a sports shirt and sorting his mail, looking for a reply from his mom. Each night, in a quiet moment, they both will say to themselves, "No word," their voices sore. Mr. Bowman probably is clambering around the foothills of the Himalayas wondering if a reply from his mom is waiting for him back home.

I step back into the tub to leave the house. Hanging from the showerhead is a wood-handled back scrubber, and I think of the day when Mr. Bowman will return from his trek, riffle his mail, and then climb in the shower, disappointed that his mother still hasn't written. His back is quilted with muscle and brown from hiking shirtless along the Sherpa paths, and under his shower-head he'll run the brush's bristles up and down the furrow of flesh that traces his spine. He'll give himself a scrub and then drift away into the sleep of night, and he will dream, and so will I.

———

At the picnic table on our patio, my mother passes a platter piled with meat patties the size of silver dollars. "I just love miniburg-ers." She drops one into Jane's jaws. My mother is talking about the people she knows whose lungs have become itchy or who've broken out with rashes, all the result of the malathion, she presumes. "It's no coincidence," she says. "It's Agent Orange all over." I can barely listen to her. The only thing I can think about is Mrs. Bowman's letter in my pocket. I can nearly feel it there against my thigh, throbbing like a fresh cut.

I hand off my miniburgers to Jane.

"Don't think I didn't see that, Mitchell," my mother snaps, her chin in her hand. "Don't think your mother doesn't see everything."

After dinner Boyd and I are hanging around the hydrangea bush for about an hour, but no matching cars drive by. "We need some more hubcaps," Boyd says. "We need something in the low end. Something for a Toyota. Or a Honda hubcap would get us lots of business."

"If you want a Honda, I'll get you one."

"Only if you find it. You can't rip 'em off of cars anymore."

"Why not?"

"Because that's stealing."

"What're you talking about? You've stolen lots of hubcaps."

"Not anymore."

"Since when?"

"Since Jessica told me how stupid it was. She said only little boys do things like that. And you know what? She's right."

"What about playing Hubcap?" I say. "Isn't that lying and deceiving and being mean?" A black Volkswagen putters by. "What's the difference between that and ripping off a hubcap?"

"There's a big difference. Hubcap is just a game. Ripping things off is for another crowd. Crooks. Cat burglars. Felons." Boyd breaks into the details of last night at Jessica's, and I can't believe that this is Boyd, nasty old Boyd, telling me I'm a thief. What's happened to him? But I know what's happened to him—Jessica—and when he starts telling me how she wore her wet bikini beneath her tank top, I wonder why the world has set things up so that Jessica Frank will fascinate Boyd yet leave me numb and bored. What is it about her and every other girl I know that turns me into a fourteen-year-old unlike everyone else? It used to be that in the hydrangea bush I often felt that, after all, Boyd and I were pretty much the same, and my vague longing for him and a few other guys at school—well, actually, nearly every other guy at school—really wasn't as isolating as I feared. But ever since Jessica's parents went out of town, leaving her alone, Boyd has made even our Hubcap command center another setting to point out that his life is proceeding nicely while mine is on the brink of careening out of control. He makes me feel like a drunk driver skidding across a lawn in the instant before he plows through a living room window.

Now my mother is convinced the malathion is the reason I'm not eating, and at dinner the next night I try to tell her she's wrong. "I'm fine."

"But how would you even know?" She throws a pop-up bun at Jane, who is busy chasing flies. "I'm worried about where you'll get your nutrients if you don't eat your dinner. Won't you have just one hot dog?" She's holding a long barbecue fork, and its prongs sparkle in the evening sun, winking like my mother's eye. She and I have always shared a wink as our secret gesture of love. I've never seen her wink at Charlie or my father or even Jane. When I was little she used to call me Monster, and I would walk around, skinny and awkward, thinking I would grow up to be just like her, and sometimes, as I perched on her tiny lap, my bony limbs locked around her neck and waist, I would tell her I wanted to be her exact twin. "You can be whatever you want," she'd say, and my chest would swell with relief. As I grew taller and skinnier, my mother's lap had a harder time holding me, but I would wiggle my way onto her. Finally, one day when I was eleven, she said to me, "You don't really want to be my exact twin, Mitchell. You want to marry her." With that, she neatly scooted me out of her lap for the last time and then called over Jane, who, though slobbering and huger than me, took my warmed place. Stunned, I looked in my mother's face for an explanation, for our wink, but she was already focused on brushing the oil out of Jane's coat and never noticed me slink away.

"Mitchell? I'm sick with worry, so I'm just going to come out and ask it: Are you having trouble with girls? Is that why you're not eating?"

"I know you don't think of me as a smooth operator, Mitch," my father pipes in, chewing his bun. "But I do know a few things about girls and their ways."

"So do I!" says my mom.

Right at this moment, in the glow of dusk, when the retreating smog stings the eyes, I consider asking my parents for help. As I watch them butter their corn and douse their hot dogs in relish and stare at me—eyes so dull and brown that they resemble a mole on the skin—I think just maybe I should split myself open and tell them what has happened. I could explain how Boyd was taking in Mr. Bowman's mail and how something about his house forced me to do things I knew were wrong even as I was doing them, how it's hard being different from Boyd and Charlie and all the other guys and all the other girls and even different from all the grown-ups I know in the world, being the most un-wanted thing that each of them can imagine, that I can imagine, and everything in my life would be okay if it weren't for this one thing, which consumes me more and more every day, and what would they do if they were me, what would they do?

"If it's about a girl, talk to us," my dad says, a smile around his ear of corn. "Or maybe it's about a couple of girls!" Then something in his square face—its similarity to my own, per-haps—tells me they can't help me, that I'll have to go it alone, that it would be much, much better if I don't bring this up with them or anyone because this is the one thing they, all of them, everyone I know, cannot, will not understand.

———

A few days later I'm waiting for Boyd in the hydrangea when he pushes his way through the leaves, red-faced and puffing.

"Why were you running?"

"Jessica's mom nearly caught me and her going at it behind their garage." Mr. and Mrs. Frank returned from their vacation two days ago, and Boyd has been moaning about it ever since. "What a fucking mess! We were back there and Jessica had her blouse open and my zipper was down and all of a sudden we hear footsteps rustling through the leaves and somebody is get-ting near and then Mrs. Frank calls out, 'Jessica? What's going on?'" Boyd is lying on his back and his T-shirt is pushed up, ex-posing the shallow cove of his belly button. "I didn't know what to do, so I just grabbed Jessica's arm and practically pulled her over the back fence with me, but shit, she got scraped up pretty bad. I told her to go home and tell her mom she fell off her bike and then I ran over here. The whole thing sucks."

"Maybe you guys should take it easy for a while."

Boyd turns his head to me. Then he snorts, his lips twisting. "Easy for you to say."

Again I want to ask him what he means, but his likely answer scares me. He could confront me here and now, I fear, but what would I do, what would I do as he calls me a fag, a homo? I could take my first step toward coming clean about Mrs. Bowman's letter if I look at him right now and say, *What do you mean by that? Tell me what you mean. I dare you* . . . But I know I'll deny it, every bit of it, and swear on my life that he's wrong, more wrong than he's ever been.

Then suddenly the clicking sound of an engine comes drifting from down the road. Boyd sits up. "Mitch! What's that?"

"Sounds like a diesel."

"That's not just a plain old diesel." He begins to crouch. "That's no lawn mower, Mitch. That's a Mercedes. It's a fucking Mercedes!"

"You sure?"

"Sure, I'm sure. You watch. We've got this one. Meet me back in front of my house, because this one's going to fly. It's going to be beautiful, man."

He stands up but not all the way, so his head won't stick out of the bush. He's gripping his hubcap between thumb and forefinger, readying it. The coughing diesel is making its way down San Rafael, and as it curves the bend we see, sure enough, it's a late-eighties night-blue Mercedes sedan driven by a lady who looks old. The car passes us. Just as we see its rear license plate, Boyd whips the hubcap through the leaves and sends it Frisbee-like through the air. It lands in the middle of the street behind the car and scrapes across the asphalt, two sparks shooting out.

The car's brake lights burn red. Boyd hops out of the bush and begins waving his hands, shouting, "Hey, lady! Your hubcap!

Your hubcap!" He runs to the hubcap, which is twirling on its rim like a quarter, and lifts it over his head. "Your hubcap! Look!"

The Mercedes' door opens and out comes the driver, visoring her hand above her eyes. She's wearing a purple-and-silver jogging suit and a ruby cocktail ring. She's confused, with her mouth hanging open. "What's going on?"

Boyd is jumping up and down. "Your hubcap came off!" he shouts. "Look, it just flew off! Here it is."

"My goodness," the lady says, her hands patting her poof of red hair.

"It just popped off," Boyd continues, still bouncing on his feet.

"Why, thank you. I heard that terrible scraping noise and I thought what on earth? Aren't you nice to stop me like this. I wonder why it fell off, but anyway, thank you so—"

And then, according to plan, Boyd begins running away with the hubcap under his arm.

"Wait a minute! Where are you going? Where are you going with my hubcap? You come back here!"

The woman starts chasing Boyd, her fist raised and her breasts bouncing back and forth like tetherballs. Eventually she stops and watches Boyd sprint to the end of the block. Then he's gone. I know he's used our regular escape route up a lemon tree and then along the brick wall of Mr. Trader's property to the opposite side of the block.

The woman stands in the middle of the street, panting. Behind her the car door hangs open, its engine idling. She sets her hands on her hips and returns to her car to examine her wheels. First the front two, then the rear, and when she arrives at the fourth intact tire she cries out, "What the hell's going on here?"

I can't wait to report to Boyd his Hubcap success. I'm desperate to share something with him, something laced with emotion, and this looks like the best chance I'll get for a while.

I meet him in his driveway, where he's sitting cross-legged on the cement, hidden behind his mom's minivan. A two-liter bottle of Coke pokes out between his legs, a drop of sweat moves down his cheek. "I got her, man."

"She was really pissed. You should've seen her."

"How pissed?"

"She was talking to herself and I heard her say she was going to call the police. Then she got on her cell phone, so I think she actually did call the police. It was awesome."

"Did she see you?"

"I don't think so."

"What'd she do when I took off?"

I tell him about the lady's confused reaction, emphasizing the corny details like her ass sticking out when she bent over to investigate. I start to make up a part about her farting, but just then Jessica appears at my side.

"Hi." She's not really looking at me.

"Jessica!" Boyd jumps up. "Did your mom figure anything out?"

"I don't think so." Band-Aids on her knees, and her hair is yanked into a ponytail, making her look even taller than she is, which is taller than either of us.

"Jessica," I say. "We just nailed a blue Mercedes in Hubcap. Totally tricked the driver!"

"Look, Boyd," she says, glancing around. "Can we go inside?"

"Yeah, sure. Catch you later, Mitch." The screen door slams.

I head back to the hydrangea to deposit the hubcap. For some reason, I know it's over: Our last round of Hubcap has come and gone, and Boyd's stash will rest now in the underbrush of the hydrangea. Through the seasons, there they'll remain, rusting and shifting deeper into the soil, undiscovered for a year or two or more, until Mr. Trader's gardener takes on the special project of cutting back the shrubbery along his wall. It's over, and I am alone, and then I lift my eyes from my feet and there, not fifty yards down the street, coming toward me, is a police car. I haven't noticed what street I'm on, but I start running. It isn't the hubcap in my hand that I'm so worried about. All I can think about is getting caught and a police officer emptying my pockets. He'd find Mrs. Bowman's letter, and that would be the end of it, everything would crash around me, and maybe I'd get out of the hubcap charge but I'd be booked on burglary and mail theft. Oh, how did it come to this, and I keep running, faster and faster, faster than ever, frightened as my lungs heave and my face slickens. Boyd will never understand how this has happened; no one will understand.

I make it back to the fancier part of the neighborhood. I'm not sure where I am, but at last I see a tall box hedge I know how to cut through. At its base there's a hole where the branches thin, and I tunnel through it and then sneak along a wall covered in passion-fruit vine, the estate of a widow. I jump the back fence choked with oleander and crawl my way across three more backyards, from swingset to doghouse to pool cabana, until I find a woodpile to hide behind.

Until late afternoon I wait there, guilty from Boyd's deed, with his hubcap locked between my knees. And as I wait for the safety of night, my heart knocking with terror, I read over and over Mrs. Bowman's letter. Only with the cover of dusk do I realize what I must do next, and so I return to Mr. Bowman's bathroom window. Once in the house—still so cool, still a foreign world—I don't waste any time. I find Mr. Bowman's bedroom down the hall. It's in his bedroom, I know.

A green spread covers the bed, a down pillow dented with the impression of a head. There's a potted tree, a trunk of gear: tennis racket, diving mask, basketball, Rollerblades, lifting gloves. There's a black dresser, and on top of it a stack of Mr. Bowman's CEO business cards, a column of pennies in an ashtray from a hotel in Tokyo, and a photo of a man propped on a sofa reading a book, soft yellow ringlets of hair falling in his eyes. With his wire glasses and the concentration on his face, and the strong heft of his arms pressing through his T-shirt, I recognize the man as Mr. Bowman, and I feel as though I've met him long ago and something important, like affection, has passed between us.

A drawer is open: rolls of socks and squares of handkerchiefs. I finger them and cautiously pull open a second drawer. Mr. Bowman's boxer shorts: green tennis rackets, orange Japanese fans, a pair with a map of Missouri on the seat. And don't you hate it when people ask you why you've done something stupid? I hate it that people think there actually is a *why*. Why don't people know that things don't happen that way? Most of the time we don't make decisions; we just act, and then the next thing we know there's a mess at our feet, and I say this now because the next thing I'm doing is dropping my shorts, and in the mirror on Mr. Bowman's closet door I see myself with my pants down. My legs are skinny, hairier than at the start of the summer, now maybe even as hairy as Boyd's. And my briefs are too tight, I see, and I don't know if this is good or bad, and I'm dirty from the chase, sweet grime in the fold of my elbow.

Who am I? I know, but nobody else except Mr. Bowman would if they were to come across me like this. I'm trying to make things as right as I can get them for Mr. Bowman and his mother, and for me. And yet it seems entirely possible that the next thing that will occur on the face of the earth will be the flash of the judging world's camera bulb, capturing me in an inaccurately guilt-loaded shot: the hubcap-stealing, trespassing boy, shorts around his ankles, lifted letter in the pocket, sex swollen and leaking, his hand caught in the underwear drawer.

I replace my briefs with a pair of Mr. Bowman's boxers. Golden roasted chickens, steam rising off the crispy skin. Funny shorts for a man, but someone probably gave them to Mr. Bowman and he doesn't care. Big in the waist and thighs, the shorts' roominess pleases me. I like the air on my skin, and I am excited, but I haven't slipped on Mr. Bowman's underwear for the same reason Boyd visits Jessica. No, there's another reason. What would Mr. Bowman want me to do about the letter? In his boxer shorts, in his bedroom, with the dust bunnies swirling in the corner from a draft coming from somewhere—but where?—maybe I can sort this out.

And so I come to realize that Mr. Bowman and I will become friends out of this, that we will look at each other and think, Me too, me too. And as I lie on the floorboards in the long shadow of his bed, my eyes staring at the ceiling, I can see the potential of something, of something shaking itself into sight for the first time.

Eventually I stand up, and I have a plan. I sit at his desk and turn on the computer. Here he probably wrote the letter to his mother, and here I'll write him a letter. I'll print it out, paper-clip it to his mother's, and leave them both in his underwear drawer. It's as simple as that, and nothing in my life has ever seemed so clear: There's the pasture, serene in angled light, white moths descending with dusk; calm returns; the day falls away.

On the blank screen the letters I type appear, explaining who I am and how I ended up in his house reading his mail. Unfolding the story, I want to tell him how I hadn't planned any of it. I want to apologize, except I'm not really sorry, I'm just respectful of his privacy. But I know he will understand. I know he could have been me, he was once me.

Mr. Bowman's house no longer feels cool. The bedroom has trapped the heat, it's trapped my heat, and as I type, hunched on his cane-bottom chair, sweat spreads across the small of my back and between my legs. My fingers continue to type as the night slides on and my palms grow damp. The first page of my tale, then the second, then the fifth burns on Mr. Bowman's computer screen. A numbness creeps into my curved back, but I don't slow to straighten myself. It's getting late. No, it's already late, and I still haven't gotten to the part how I thought about showing Mrs. Bowman's letter to my own mother, hoping we could use it as a model of how a mother and her son can work things out. How I might have really done it, too, if Michele hadn't pulled up the driveway and dumped dumb, drunk Charlie at our door.

I continue writing, the pressure of time and heat closing in on my opportunity to report all that has occurred. In the summer sky I hear the thudding whir—at first distant and soft, then approaching and menacing, just like in the movies—of the medfly helicopter brigade aerosoling the neighborhood with fog banks of malathion. The whipping blades tell me I'm late getting home and that Jane is now whimpering in the backyard. But I can't stop, not yet. My head peers over the keyboard, the tendons in my neck tight. My wrists stiffen with ache. My fingers type even faster, misspelling almost every other word, but I still need to tell Mr. Bowman how he can contact me so we can meet, and just at this moment I hear a noise from the kitchen door, and my fingers stop, skip a beat, but then begin typing again. I am nearly finished, and the letter can explain it better: I can imagine the words gagging in my throat. It's all in the letter, I'll say. Footsteps move down the hall, and I hunker closer to the computer screen. I imagine Mr. Bowman's blocky face will first screw up in confusion, but then it will relax with sympathy. "What's going on here?" he'll ask gently, rubbing my neck, somehow knowing how I ended up in his house, at his desk, in his underwear. I crane my neck to see the door frame, my fingers still typing, and just as Boyd and Jessica tiptoe forward and squint into the gray computer glow of their borrowed love nest, their dewy faces stuck in the silent instant between rosy excitement and ashen disgust, just at this moment, when before I would have felt only the tent of my soul collapse, just at this moment I realize that I am no more evil than Boyd, that if he can seek pleasure so will I, and that passion for us all will remain a troublesome thing.

ACKNOWLEDGMENTS

Over the years, many people read some or all of these stories, in early and late draft, each editing in his or her uniquely subtle way: Daphne Beal, Marc Olmstead, Ron Kraft, Melanie Bishop, Brian Bouldrey, Michael Lowenthal, David Nichols, Susan Monsky, Neenyah Ostrom, Jennifer Marshall, Kevin McIlvoy, Hilton Als. David Bergman, godfather to many of us, read several stories early on and always said, soothingly, send more. My editor at Weidenfeld & Nicholson in London, Rebecca Wilson, shaped the final manuscript with her expert pencil. Carole McCurdy copyedited the manuscript with exactitude and care. Thanks also to my friends at Viking Penguin: Gretchen Koss; Paul Slovak; my editor, Ray Roberts; Kathryn Court; Patrick Nolan; Cliff Corcoran. I remain grateful to Barbara Grossman and Jonathan Burnham for first signing me up.

Finally, I owe much to my agent, Elaine Koster; she is the best of representatives: a writer's friend.

FOR THE BEST IN PAPERBACKS, LOOK FOR THE

In every corner of the world, on every subject under the sun, Penguin represents quality and variety—the very best in publishing today.

For complete information about books available from Penguin—including Puffins, Penguin Classics, and Compass—and how to order them, write to us at the appropriate address below. Please note that for copyright reasons the selection of books varies from country to country.

In the United Kingdom: Please write to *Dept. EP, Penguin Books Ltd, Bath Road, Harmondsworth, West Drayton, Middlesex UB7 0DA.*

In the United States: Please write to *Penguin Putnam Inc., P.O. Box 12289 Dept. B, Newark, New Jersey 07101-5289* or call 1-800-788-6262.

In Canada: Please write to *Penguin Books Canada Ltd, 10 Alcorn Avenue, Suite 300, Toronto, Ontario M4V 3B2.*

In Australia: Please write to *Penguin Books Australia Ltd, P.O. Box 257, Ringwood, Victoria 3134.*

In New Zealand: Please write to *Penguin Books (NZ) Ltd, Private Bag 102902, North Shore Mail Centre, Auckland 10.*

In India: Please write to *Penguin Books India Pvt Ltd, 11 Panchsheel Shopping Centre, Panchsheel Park, New Delhi 110 017.*

In the Netherlands: Please write to *Penguin Books Netherlands bv, Postbus 3507, NL-1001 AH Amsterdam.*

In Germany: Please write to *Penguin Books Deutschland GmbH, Metzlerstrasse 26, 60594 Frankfurt am Main.*

In Spain: Please write to *Penguin Books S. A., Bravo Murillo 19, 1° B, 28015 Madrid.*

In Italy: Please write to *Penguin Italia s.r.l., Via Benedetto Croce 2, 20094 Corsico, Milano.*

In France: Please write to *Penguin France, Le Carré Wilson, 62 rue Benjamin Baillaud, 31500 Toulouse.*

In Japan: Please write to *Penguin Books Japan Ltd, Kaneko Building, 2-3-25 Koraku, Bunkyo-Ku, Tokyo 112.*

In South Africa: Please write to *Penguin Books South Africa (Pty) Ltd, Private Bag X14, Parkview, 2122 Johannesburg.*